WABI

A HERO'S TALE

Joseph Bruchac

DIAL BOOKS

DIAL BOOKS
A member of Penguin Group (USA) Inc.
Published by The Penguin Group
Penguin Group (USA) Inc., 375 Hudson Street, New York, NY 10014, U.S.A.
Penguin Group (Canada), 90 Eglinton Avenue East, Suite 700, Toronto, Ontario, Canada M4P 2Y3 (a division of Pearson Penguin Canada Inc.)
Penguin Books Ltd, 80 Strand, London WC2R 0RL, England
Penguin Ireland, 25 St. Stephen's Green, Dublin 2, Ireland
(a division of Penguin Books Ltd)
Penguin Group (Australia), 250 Camberwell Road, Camberwell, Victoria 3124, Australia (a division of Pearson Australia Group Pty Ltd)
Penguin Books India Pvt Ltd, 11 Community Centre, Panchsheel Park, New Delhi - 110 017, India
Penguin Group (NZ), Cnr Airborne and Rosedale Roads, Albany, Auckland 1310, New Zealand (a division of Pearson New Zealand Ltd)
Penguin Books (South Africa) (Pty) Ltd, 24 Sturdee Avenue, Rosebank, Johannesburg 2196, South Africa
Penguin Books Ltd, Registered Offices: 80 Strand, London WC2R 0RL, England

Book designed by Jasmin Rubero
Text set in Adobe Garamond
Printed in the U.S.A.

10 9 8 7 6 5 4 3 2 1

Library of Congress Cataloging-in-Publication Data
Bruchac, Joseph, date.
Wabi : a hero's tale / Joseph Bruchac.
p. cm.
Summary: After falling in love with an Abenaki Indian woman, a white great horned owl named Wabi transforms into a human being and has several trials and adventures while learning to adapt to his new life.
ISBN 0-8037-3098-5
1. Abenaki Indians—Fiction. [1. Abenaki Indians—Fiction. 2. Great horned owl—Fiction. 3. Owls—Fiction. 4. Indians of North America—Fiction.] I. Title.
PZ7.B82816Wab 2006
[Fic]—dc22
2005015392

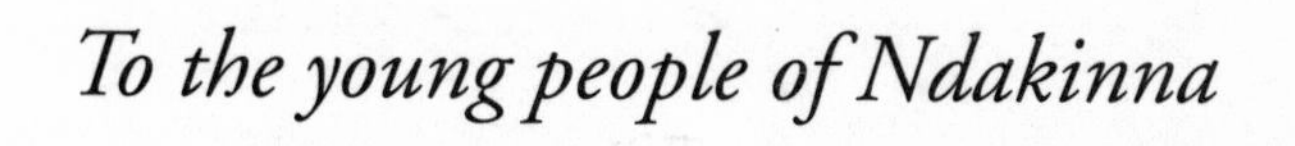

To the young people of Ndakinna

Contents

WABI

CHAPTER 1

First Memories

I ALMOST DIED BEFORE I could fly. That is what I remember most about when I was little.

It's not the first thing I remember. The first thing was feeling surrounded by a wall that was wrapped around me. The wall had never bothered me before. I'd always felt warm and secure. But then a frantic feeling came over me. I had to get out of there. I pushed against the wall with my head, attacked it with my beak. Finally, when it seemed as if I couldn't fight any longer, I broke through.

My brother was waiting for me on the other side. He is the second thing I remember. Unfortunately. He gave me a big shove. Then he bit me.

"That hurt!" I said.

"Get used to it," he replied.

Actually, what I said was, "Hrttt-rrrrllll!" And what he said back to me was, "Hrrllll." Then he bit me again.

There wasn't much I could do to fight back. I was really little. You wouldn't think it to look at me now, but I was the smallest one in my family. My sister and brother were both bigger than me.

My sister never paid much attention to me. She had bigger things to worry about, namely our brother. But I learned a lot from her, just by watching. I saw how she could sidestep to keep out of my brother's way when our mother wasn't around. I started doing the same thing and began to avoid most of his pecks and pushes. When our mother came back, my brother ignored us. He was too interested in seeing what food she brought and making sure that he got most of it.

"KURRULLL, KURRULLL, KURRULLL," he would shriek, opening his mouth as wide as he could and shouldering us aside.

What he said meant: "Mine, mine, mine!"

That was pretty much it as far as the food our mother brought to us. From the half-digested bits of yummy little critters that she coughed up when we were owlets to the nice crunchy whole mice that hung limp and delicious from her beak as we got older, my big brother always got more than my sister and me.

Of course I got the least. That is what happens when you are the last one to hatch.

My sister kept her eyes open for anything else that might be dangerous. Lots of creatures like to eat little owls. She was always looking up, looking down, turning her head around. I learned to do that too. Or at least I did so when I wasn't sidestepping as fast as I could to keep away from my big brother's beak. The only good thing about his eating more than us was that it also meant he slept more.

Keeping very quiet and still was also something my big sister did really well, especially when the shadow of another wide-winged bird went over. Being silent is useful in other ways than avoiding the attention of a hungry hawk or crow. For one, it makes you a better listener. Listening is very, very important. When you are small, you can hear things that might eat you. When you are grown, it's the other way around.

Although I learned a lot from her, I know that my big sister wasn't trying to teach me. She acted as if I didn't exist.

My brother, though, did pay attention to me. Unfortunately.

"Whoool-tooo, Rrrtrrbrrll!" Move, Runt!

"Grrraaaccc!" Drop that food!

"Hrrllll." Get used to it.

I'm not sure how I survived. From other owls, I've learned that every nest was not as bad as ours. In most nests, the chicks squabble a little around feeding time, but otherwise just live and let live. It was just my luck to have been hatched into one with an ornicidal maniac.

I remember waking up one night from a dream in which our whole tree was being shaken by a big scary wind. I was being thrown around, all right, but not by the wind. The next violent push against me made me realize two things real fast. The first, of course, was that my brother was the one shoving me. The second realization was that I had been pushed up onto the edge of the nest. I was about to fall.

I didn't know for sure what was down there. I'd never

touched the earth or seen things like grass and flowers close up. My whole world was our nest and the branches around us, the sky, and my mother's wide wings overhead. There was also, every now and then, another presence in the high branches of the tree some distance from ours. It wasn't threatening, like the crows our mother warned us about.

"Black-wings come in, they eat you then," was what she said. Things that wanted to devour tender little owlets made up a good part of her conversations. "Don't get eaten," was the only advice she ever gave us.

But even though that distant presence seemed to me to be another owl rather than a crow, it never came close to feed us the way our mother did.

At the moment when my brother had shoved me to the very edge of our nest, I didn't think about that other owl. All I could think was that I was about to be pushed out.

I grabbed the side of the nest with both feet, dug my claws in hard, and shoved back at my brother. To my surprise, he yelped and went rolling into the center of the nest. He landed on his back and stayed there, threatening me with his claws.

I ignored him as I hopped down to safety. Even though I was small, I was tougher than I'd thought. Was I stronger than my big brother? It was an interesting thought. All the rest of that day he didn't push me or nip me even once. He clacked his beak a time or two, but I could live with that. Especially as opposed to being pushed out to fall to what I suspected was certain death below. Foxes, weasels, wolverines, wolves, minks, fishers, bears, snakes. Our mother had mentioned all of them as well as a few more creatures that were even larger, scarier, and just as likely to view a little owl as a nice snack in between bigger meals. "Monsters," she said. "They want to eat you."

The thought of being strong enough to actually defend myself made me feel self-confident. I wasn't used to feeling confident. Hungry, uncertain, wary, confused, disappointed, and bruised, yes. But not confident.

It turned out that being confident was not as good a thing as I thought. I felt so self-confident that I stopped watching my brother as closely as I had been. Instead, when my mother fed us the next day, I hopped forward, beak open, and got a limp fat mouse all to myself. As I gulped it down, I watched her spread her wings and float into flight. It looked easy. I'd never thought about being able to fly before. I hopped over to the edge of the nest and peered up as she sailed away.

I could do that someday, I thought, extending one wing to look at it. My feathers had been growing in nicely. Not one bit of yellow fluff was left.

Then something hit me hard from behind.

My brother had seen his chance. My feet grabbed at the small sticks that edged our nest, but I was too late. I had been pushed right out. I was falling.

"RRTTTTBLLL!" my brother hooted triumphantly as I plummeted. Down I went, down, down toward the deadly ground below.

CHAPTER 2

Falling

MY DROP COULD NOT HAVE taken long, but it didn't seem that short to me. I had far too much time to think about far too many things as the wind of my fall whistled past me.

Our mother had warned us so many times about what was down there that it seemed to me impossible I could survive. "Stumps and stones will break all your bones," she would burble whenever she saw one of us even leaning toward the edge of the nest to try and look over.

And if getting all my bones broken didn't kill me, that would not be the end of it. I could then look forward to some hungry creature coming to eat me up.

All of that might have happened if I had just kept tumbling, beak over tail. But at some point I remembered those new wing feathers that I had been admiring.

Birds don't fall, a voice inside my head said. *They fly.*

I thrust my wings open. It stopped my descent almost as suddenly as a spider coming to a halt in midair at the end of its silk thread. Almost. You see, I didn't stop completely. Opening my wings just turned my plummeting fall into a slow glide. Slow enough for me to realize I was heading right toward a big pine tree whose lower branches had died and broken off, leaving stubs that looked as sharp as fangs. If I ran into one, I would be impaled. I wouldn't have to worry then about hungry predators. I would already be dead meat!

I tried wildly to remember how my mother looked when she flew. What was it that she did to stop or change directions as she came in to land? Feet out, shoulders hunched up—that was it. I thrust my legs forward and shrugged my shoulders. It worked! Not only did I slow down, I managed to turn away from the pine tree entirely.

But in my excitement, I thrust my feet and flapped just a little too hard.

Whooops! I flipped backward in midair and landed—if you can call it that—totally upside down. I hadn't struck any of those stumps or stones my mother had warned about, but I had been introduced to something else that wasn't exactly friendly. Blackberry bushes. Their thorns had grasped me as firmly as a wasp stuck in pine sap.

I thrashed around trying to work free. All that it did was make those thorns stick even more firmly into my feathers. I was caught, even though the top of my head was less than a wing's width from the ground.

"That was a very impressive landing," a friendly voice said from somewhere behind me. "Yes, it was. Yes, indeed."

I tried to turn toward the voice. Usually that would be an easy thing for an owl to do. Our eyes don't move in our heads the way human eyes do, but we can turn our heads all the way around on our necks to look behind us. However, the stubborn blackberry thorns held me tight. Being upside down was bad enough. Not being able to look around made me even more nervous.

"Ah," the friendly voice continued. "You cannot turn your little head around to see me? Do not worry. I will make it easy for you to see me. Yes, I will."

Owls have very big ears. We can hear such things as a vole shuddering in the dry leaves at the base of an oak that is twenty trees away. So even though the one who was talking to me moved softly, I heard every footstep that he made. It was the sound of someone who was used to creeping up on the unwary.

I clacked my beak in frustration. I had a feeling that I knew what I was about to see and that I would be no match for it. But if I just had my wings and talons free, I could at least put up a fight.

"Here I am," that voice said, a voice that I now realized was not friendly at all. It was pleased. And hungry.

"Here I am. Yes, here I am, indeed," said the red-coated animal that smiled down at me. "As you can see, I am a fox, yes. Are you glad to see me? I am glad, yes, very glad to see you."

The fox slid closer. He was so close that I could feel his hot breath on my beak. He opened his mouth wide. His teeth looked longer and sharper than the broken branches of that pine tree.

CHAPTER 3
Little Food

I KNEW VERY LITTLE ABOUT life outside our nest. But as that fox's mouth opened even wider, I realized that I had now learned two new things. The first was that foxes have very bad breath. The second was that my own life was apparently going to be very short.

I didn't like what was about to happen at all. It wasn't having my little hollow bones crunched between those drooling jaws that bothered me the most, although I certainly didn't look forward to it. It was being unable to do anything about it. Even more than to escape, I wanted to fight back.

I clacked my beak again and struggled against the blackberry thorns. I was so agitated that I was actually able to free one of my legs. Without hesitation, I thrust my foot out toward my enemy's face, claws first. To my surprise, my long middle talon poked the fox right in his black nose.

"YOWP!" The fox jumped back and shook his head. He was even more surprised than I was. A little drop of red appeared on the tip of his nose.

"Little Food, why did you do that?" the fox growled. "Yes, why? I held no resentment toward you, no. I was feeling quite fond of you before you did that. Why, yes, why?"

I didn't answer. There was no point, really. I just kept my eyes on him and my one free foot ready.

"Ah," the fox said, the grin coming back onto his face, "the Little Food does not answer me. I was just going to eat him in one quick gulp, yes. But now I think I will first pull out all his feathers. Then I will eat him just one little bite at a time. Yes, I will."

He took a step toward me and I thrust my talons out at him again. This time, though, he stepped back before I could make contact.

"Oh, how sweet. The Little Food likes to fight," the fox said. His voice was amused again. "But he is still stuck in the thorny, thorny bushes. Yes, he is. He will not be able to see me if I go behind him. No. So that is what I will do. Yes, yes, I will."

The fox began to move off to one side, as smooth as rainwater flowing down the trunk of a tree. I tried to follow him with my eyes, but he was right. I was caught so tightly I could not turn my body. A few more steps and he was out of my line of vision.

"Hrrgrrrblll, hrrrgrrblll!" I said. "Unfair, unfair!"

But even though I could no longer see the fox, I could still hear him. Not that it did me any good. My ears picked up every stealthy footstep, the sound of his slow breathing, even the beating of his heart. Then, though I was not completely certain, I thought I heard something else too. Something that was not the fox.

"Now, what shall I do first to the Little Food?" said the self-satisfied fox. "Shall I pull out his tail feathers and show them to him one by one? Yes, I will do that."

"Ahem," said another, deeper voice. "Are you sure that is what you will dooo?"

That second voice too came from behind me. I could not see who was speaking. But my owl ears told me that this other being was both large and looking down at the fox as it spoke to him.

"Eeep," the fox said. His voice was not at all self-satisfied now. I could hear his heart beat faster.

"Well?" said that deep voice again.

"Ah," the fox said, his feet moving him backward and away from me as he spoke. "Ah, that is, I mean to say not at all. No, not at all. And now, yes, now I have remembered that I must go somewhere else. Yes, I must go. Right now!"

There was the sound of feet scrabbling in the leaves as the fox made a rapid turn and started to run. Then there was a bonking sound and an "Ouch!" as the fox's head hit the tree behind him. More frantic sounds of fleeing fox feet followed.

"Excuse me," the deep voice said. "I think he still needs a little reminder about who is food and whooo is not."

Then came a sound that I knew well.

Fwoomp, fwoomp, fwoomp, fwoomp.

It was the soft beat of wings that would be silent to any other than owl ears. And next came a more distant, but louder, noise.

"YOWP!"

My ears showed me the picture of a fox being lifted up into the air.

"No, I say, no. Put me down. Not from this high, no. Yooowwp."

Whomp!

The thud of the fox hitting the ground after being dropped was followed, after a brief silence, by the sound of a fox trying to skulk away quietly, despite the necessity of having to limp while doing so.

Fwoomp, fwoomp, fwoomp, fwoomp.

The wingbeats came back again and then the flying creature landed in front of me. Even upside down I could see that it was another owl. It was not my mother, but an older owl.

I could also see that this new owl had a friendly look on her face and the tip of a fox's tail hanging from her beak.

"Great-grandson," she said in a warm, deep voice, dropping the piece of fur to one side as she spoke, "let us get you out of those briars."

CHAPTER 4
Who?

UPSIDE DOWN I STARED AT that big owl. "Who? Who? Whooo are you?" I said, full of suspicion.

"Little one," she whootuled, "doooo not worry. I am your great-grandmother."

Great-grandmother?

I wasn't sure what that meant. And as she hopped closer to me, what I noticed most was how big and sharp her beak and her claws looked. Sure, she had just driven off that fox. But maybe she had only saved me so she could eat me herself.

I knew that big birds ate smaller birds. We had learned that early on from my mother. Hawks, crows, blue jays, those were all on my mother's endless list of horrors. It seemed as if everything in the world equated nestlings with lunch.

And aside from my mother, I'd never seen another grown

owl close-up before. I know now that usually both the mother and father bring food to their owlets, but my mother had always done it all by herself and I'd never thought to ask where my father had gone. She probably would not have told me. My mother never talked about the past. Just "eat this," "beware of that."

So, as that big owl hopped even closer, I stuck out my free foot again and clacked my beak. In response, she laughed. Yes, owls can laugh. I hadn't known that until then, so I am not sure why the laughter touched me the way it did. Somehow I knew it was a friendly sound. Somehow I knew that it meant she was pleased with me.

"Huutttullllulll, huuttuullull," my great-grandmother laughed. "You are a brave one, my little Wabi."

Wabi? I'd never been called that before. The only name I'd ever known was Runt. *Wabi.* I liked that. I pulled my leg back in.

One more hop and my great-grandmother's head was right next to mine. She gently nuzzled the base of my neck with her beak. It felt good. Now and then, but never often enough, my mother had done that to me.

I was caught good and tight. It took a lot of pulling and twisting and snipping of that blackberry bush to free me. It wasn't easy, and I know that more than once those long thorns must have drawn blood from her as she worked. But she didn't stop or slow down her steady pace. There was a job to do and she would get it done. I learned later that this was the way my great-grandmother did everything in her long life. She would always study a situation before making a decision, but once she was certain, nothing could stop her. That care and determination were two of the reasons why she was older than any other owl.

Finally there was only one more thorn holding me. She bent it with one foot, then leaned forward to tug with her beak.

SNAP!

It broke free and so did I. I landed—PLOP—right on my back. Instinctively, as soon as I felt the earth beneath me, I spread out my wings and thrust both feet up, claws spread wide.

"Huutttullllulll, huuttuullull," my great-grandmother laughed again. "Wabi is ready to fight. But there is nooo need for that now. You are safe with me."

Again, somehow, I knew that was so. I pulled my legs back in, folded my wings, and rolled up to my feet. I lifted my head to look up at my great-grandmother as she leaned over and nuzzled me again. And I felt something I had never really felt before in my brief harried life. I felt happy.

CHAPTER 5

First Flight

"GO TO SLEEP, WABI," MY great-grandmother whootuled down to me softly.

She was perched just above me, on a sturdy branch of the small hemlock. This tree's branches came down to the ground so thickly that it was impossible for any hungry creature to see the small owl crouched at the base of the tree, half asleep on a soft, dry cushion of needles. But my great-grandmother was not half asleep, even though the red eye of the Day Fire—which is what we owls call the sun—was now glowing bright. Her eyes were only partly open because of the bright daylight, but they were watchful. I looked up at her one more time and then closed my eyes to drift off into a peaceful sleep.

By now you must have realized that my great-grandmother was not like every other owl. Caring for a little one not directly your own was not the usual behavior of an owl. Not only had she spent half the night hunting for food to feed my hungry mouth, she had found this safe spot for me to hide until my wings were strong enough to fly.

It is true that some mother birds keep feeding their little ones when they fall from the nest too soon. My own mother, though, was not one of those. Out of nest, out of mind was her way. Gone is forgotten.

I suppose I can understand that when I consider the fact that my mother was caring for us all by herself. It was probably hard for her to think of anything other than finding enough food. And my mother was not a thinker. Listen, fly, grab, gulp, then do it all over again until the bright eye in the sky comes back. Then sleep and dream about listening, flying, grabbing, and gulping. That was my mother's entire life, aside from the brief time she'd spent with my father.

Great-grandmother, who for sure was one who thought of many things, explained that to me when I asked her why my mother didn't do a better job of caring for me.

"Do not be angry at her, Wabi," she cooed to me. "She does not know much."

Then she told me I was more like my father, her grandson. Not in thinking. He wasn't much at that or he never would have ended up with my mother. But in courage.

"Your father," Great-grandmother said, "never feared anything, nooo, not him." Then she shook her head sadly.

As the beautiful light of the night traveler, the moon, shone each night, my great-grandmother kept feeding and preening me. She faithfully kept watch over me during each day. The moon grew from a thin arc to a full round face during that time. I grew too. More than I had ever grown before. Not having to compete with a greedy brother made a difference.

Finally, as I flapped my wings in that little sheltering place under our hemlock, I felt that I was ready.

"I want to try," I said. "Now, now. I want to fly!"

My great-grandmother pushed a branch aside with her shoulder. I hopped out, and jumped and flapped hard at the same time.

And I flew! I flew strong and straight! I flapped again and again and... I ran right into the trunk of a white birch tree.

Whomp! Flop!

I was on my back on the ground again. My feathers had cushioned the blow and I wasn't hurt, but I was angry. I jumped up and glared at that birch tree, lowered my head, lifted my wings and . . . then thought better of it. It would not do any good to fight with a tree. It hadn't tried to knock me down. I had flown into it. I lowered my wings and swiveled my head around to look at my great-grandmother, who had just landed behind me.

"Goooood," she said. Her voice sounded happy.

"That was *not* a good flight," I said. I was not happy. "You saw me run into that tree."

Great-grandmother chuckled. "That is true," she said. "But I was not talking about your flight. It is good that you did not attack that tree. Your father ran into a birch tree the first time he flew toooo. Then he spent half of the night fighting with it. He clawed all the lower bark off that tree and broke one of his claws. And even when he finally saw he could not beat a tree, he made it a point to never land in a birch from then on. Wabi, it is good that you know how to think."

Her words pleased me so much that I opened my wings, flapped them, and flew again. This time I didn't fly into that tree. I shrugged one shoulder a little more than the other, as I had seen my great-grandmother do. It worked. I turned and turned. I flew in a circle around the tall birch, rising higher and higher until I landed in its topmost branch.

"I am Wabi," I called up to the face of the night traveler. "I can think."

My great-grandmother came flying up and I moved in a little to make room for her. "That is true," she called. "True, true, trooo."

CHAPTER 6
Questions

WHEN I THINK BACK ON those seasons while I was growing up, I realize how patient my great-grandmother was with me. No matter what I asked her, she always tried to give me an answer.

"Why is there day and night?" I asked her once, raising my ear tufts in an inquisitive way. We were sitting together on the high limb of a pine just as the eye of the day was vanishing.

"Hoo-too-loo, long agooo . . ." she began.

I leaned against her, fluffing out my feathers in delight. I loved it whenever she started to answer this way. It meant a story.

"Hoo-too-loo," she hooted again, "there was nothing but dark. There was darkness everywhere. There was a world then, but it was always night."

"Hooo-hooo," I said, raising my ear tufts even higher. The thought of a world where it was always night was wonderful and exciting.

"It was beautiful," my great-grandmother said. "In that world loooong ago, we flew in darkness all the time. Even the night traveler did not show her face. We hunted and flew and sang in the darkness, and it sang back to us."

"Hooo-hooo," I said again as my great-grandmother paused to let the picture of her story grow in my thoughts.

"Ooh-hoo," said great grandmother, "but although that dark was good for owls, it was not good for all things. The little ones who eat plants and grasses had no food, for their food would not grow without the light. So the Great Darkness spoke to us; it asked us to agree that there should also be light. That way the creatures that feared the darkness could survive, that way plants would be able to grow. And there was one more thing.

"'Soooon,' the Great Darkness said, 'there will be other beings here. They will walk on two legs as you owls do when you are on the ground. But they will not fly and they will be afraid of the darkness for they will not be as brave as owls. You owls,' the Great Darkness continued, 'are my best creation, I love you very much. But I ask you to sacrifice, to give up half of the beautiful night so that these pitiful new beings can also live.'"

Great-grandmother paused and looked toward the horizon where the moon was just beginning to appear.

I knew what was going to happen next in her story. It made me feel proud to be an owl. It also made me curious about those two-legged ones that were mentioned by the Great Darkness. I had not heard about them before.

"Soooo," great-grandmother said, "we owls agreed. We gave up half of the beautiful night to make day. And that is how it has been ever since."

"Hooo-hoo," I said.

I felt glad about what the Great Darkness did. Even though the brightness of day hurt my eyes, it was a good thing. Without day, we would not have so many things to eat. Those mice and rabbits and squirrels and other creatures could only grow to be fat and tasty by eating the plants that needed the light to grow.

Thinking back now to when I was sure that everything in the world had been made for us night-flyers, I have to smile at how little I really understood.

"Great-grandmother," I asked at the time, "who are those two-legged ones that the Great Darkness spoke of? Did they ever get created?"

Great-grandmother looked at me in a strange way, as if she was remembering something sad. Then she nodded her head. "Yes, Wabi. Those two-legged ones are called human beings."

"Do any of them live near us? What are they like? Can we go and see them?"

She chuckled. "You are asking tooo many questions at once, great-grandson. Yes, there are humans who live close by. And you will learn what they are like one day. I am sure of that."

I rocked back and forth from one foot to another.

"Can we go see them now?" I asked.

"Not yet, Wabi, but soooon."

I stared down at my feet, trying not to ask more questions, but it was no use. "Great-grandmother, how is it that you know so much?"

"It is because I know what I do not know, Wabi," she said to me.

I was confused. How could you know what you do not know? Did that mean knowing or not knowing? I sat staring at my feet through half the night and still didn't have an answer.

I had so many questions that I felt as if my head would burst. I could not keep quiet.

"Why do I ask so many questions?" I said to Great-grandmother one day.

"It is because you are you," she answered.

That led to another bout of foot-staring, and not just for one night. How could I be anyone else but me?

It was many winters later when I asked the question that changed everything for me. I was now the biggest owl in the whole forest. That was a surprise to me, but even more of a surprise to others. Usually female owls are bigger than males.

The question came about because of a chance meeting one night with another owl. My sister. I came across her while hunting in our far ridge one look away from my roosting place. (A look is as far as you can see while sitting in a high place. That is how we owls measure distance.)

My sister swiveled her head to look up at me when I floated down onto the branch just above her.

"Sister, hello," I said in a neutral tone.

I was determined to be polite, even if she had intruded on the hunting territory that great-grandmother and I controlled.

She fluffed up her feathers, trying to look bigger. Then she realized that she recognized my voice. She stared hard at me.

"Rrrtrrbrrll, ull-ooo?" she hooted in a confused voice. Runt, is that you?

"The name is Wabi," I said. "I am Runt no longer. What do you think of that? Are you not glad to see me?"

She didn't answer me. She just kept staring. Perhaps her narrow mind could not accept the fact that I was not only alive but bigger than she was.

She may have been surprised too at the way I looked. And here is another thing I have not mentioned before—the color of my feathers.

In every way but one, I looked like other owls of my kind—from the two tufts of feather that rise like horns on top of my head to the sharp, curved claws on my feet. In every way but one—my color. My color was not like theirs. Where their feathers were brown, mine were pale, almost the color of snow.

That was why my great-grandmother had given me the name Wabi, which means "white." By the light of the moon, especially on a night when her face was full and open as it was on the night when I met my sister again, I almost glowed.

My sister kept staring at me, her ear tufts flattened down against her head. There was no friendship in her gaze and certainly not much intelligence. I lost patience with her.

"HOO-HOO! HOOOO!" I hooted in my loudest voice, spreading my wings as I did so. "MY TERRITORY! MOVE!"

My sister did just that. She dove off the branch and flapped her wings, not in the leisurely way we do when hunting, but in panic, vanishing into the distance. She would not intrude on my hunting ground again.

I went looking for Great-grandmother. It did not take me long to find her. She was in the top of a great pine that stood not far from the place where I had just had my encounter with my unfriendly sister. She had probably seen—and heard—it all.

That was when I asked the question.

"Why didn't my sister answer me?"

Great-grandmother looked at me. It was one of those looks that told me I had to be patient and listen closely. So I did, even though I rocked back and forth from one foot to the other as I waited.

"Wabi," Great-grandmother said at last, looking out at the forest as she spoke, "she could not understand you."

"Why?"

This time I did not have to wait for the answer.

Great-grandmother turned and looked straight at me. "She could not understand because you were not speaking owl talk. You were talking as the human beings do."

"But that is how you and I talk all the time," I said. "Why do those two-legged ones speak the same words that we do?"

"Because it is the other way around," she said.

"You mean we talk to each other with human words?" It was very confusing to me. "Why is that so?"

This led to the longest silence my great-grandmother had ever forced on me. We sat there so long that my impatient rocking scraped all the bark from the branch under my feet. Moon moved almost the entire way across the sky as I waited for an answer.

My great-grandmother finally turned to me and sighed.

"Wabi," she said, "you and I have a special gift that most owls do not have. We are able, if we listen closely, to understand the speech of many other beings. Not just owls, but humans and other creatures toooo."

"Why?" I asked. As usual, one answer was not enough to satisfy me.

Great-grandmother shook her head. "On another night, I will answer you. Now the moment is not right."

Then she flew away, leaving me with even more questions for which I had no answers.

CHAPTER 7
Listening

LISTENING IS VERY IMPORTANT. EVEN the dullest owl knows that. Our survival depends on using our ears, even before we use our eyes, our wings, and our talons.

"Wabi," Great-grandmother said to me soon after she began caring for me, "always remember that you have two ears, two eyes, two wings, and two feet. But you have only one mouth."

I understood what she meant, or at least I thought I did.

Two ears to hear food. Two eyes to see it when it starts to run. Two wings to sweep down on it. Two feet to grab it firm. And then, of course, one mouth was plenty enough to eat it.

I know now that Great-grandmother meant more than that. I was asking so many questions that it probably seemed to her as if I had more than one mouth. I hadn't discovered yet that curiosity can get you into more trouble than listening and looking, flying and grabbing. But I was about to learn.

For some reason, I had decided to watch the setting of the Day Fire all by myself from a tall broken cedar at the edge of the big swamp. I had not told my great-grandmother where I was going. After all, I was a big owl now, even though I was still young. What did I have to be afraid of?

That, of course, was a question I should have been asking myself.

That night, though, as I sat there watching the colors of the sky-edge change, I was not thinking of questions. Instead I was just enjoying how it all looked. There were no owl words to express how I felt, but I had learned some new words that seemed right. Since my great-grandmother had told me we were using human words to talk with each other, I had begun to pay attention to those two-legged beings who lived near the waterfall. Some evenings I would sit hidden in a cedar tree to watch and listen and remember what they said about things. So I spoke some of those words now.

"The sky color is so pretty now," I said, and then I sighed. A bit too loudly, as it turned out. Someone else heard me.

"Young one," a quavery voice called out from deep in the swamp. "Young one, do you hearrr meeee?"

I turned my head to listen more closely to that voice. It was a voice I had never heard before. It was... strange. I might have said it was pleasant, but somehow it made me feel uneasy. Yet it was an attractive voice, a voice that made me curious. I knew immediately that I wanted to see the one who had that voice.

“Young one, come hhhhhheeeerrre,” it trilled, “into the swaaaammmp. I have something forrrrr you.”

What could it be? What did it have for me?

I turned my head way around to see if my great-grandmother was anywhere near so that I could ask her those questions. Then I remembered that I had left her two ridges away, in the valley of many cliffs. If I wanted an answer, I would have to go and see for myself.

I flew slowly toward that voice as it continued to call. My curiosity was great, yet somehow I knew that something was wrong. There was an edge to that voice that was...what? Hungry? I began to feel suspicious.

“Come a little deeeperrrr, into the swaaaamp. I have something forrrrrrr you.”

On I flew, just a little above the ground, following a trail that wound and wove farther into the swamp. If a two-legged young one had been following that voice, that little human being would have been lost long ago.

“Heeerrre, come heeeerrre,” the voice called. And then it stopped.

The trail ended. I dropped down and landed on a grassy hummock. I was a little ways back from the edge of a deep, dark pool of water. A few bubbles rose to the surface and broke, releasing a very nasty smell. Perhaps a young human being would have walked closer to that water to look into it, entranced by that voice. But not I. Now I knew for sure that something was wrong.

I had noticed a pile of rocks back around the last bend in the trail. I flew quietly back and picked up two of them. Then I flew back to hover just above the place where the trail ended and the black water began. I dropped my first rock on the trail, then the next, even closer to the water's edge. The thump of those rocks on the earth sounded like footsteps to my ears—and to the ears of someone else as well.

"ARRRRRHHHHH, I HAVE YOU!" A big shape burst up from the water. It rose so high that it almost struck me with its big head as I hovered there. I had to flap my wings and bank quickly to one side to avoid it. But it was not looking up. Its huge yellow eyes stared straight ahead at the bank as its two long-clawed hands struck at the spot where my second rock had fallen, the spot where a young human being would have been standing.

"ARHHHHHH?" the creature said, staring at its empty hands. "I don't have you?"

I had landed on the top of one of the red willows that grew at the opposite edge of the pool. My perch was four times as high as the creature had leaped, so I was fairly certain I would be safe. I cocked my head to study it. Its body was like that of one of those two-leggeds I had begun to watch all the time in their village below the great waterfall, where they lived in those peculiar nests that they built upside down and on the ground. From the shape of its body, the creature seemed to be a woman.

But this was not a human woman. It was three times as large as the biggest human I had seen. Its head was like the head of a giant toad. Its mouth was wide enough to swallow a small two-legged person whole. I knew what I was looking at. It was a true monster, one of the terrible non-animal beings that hunt humans.

My great-grandmother had told me about such creatures. Back when the world was formed, some creatures had come out wrong. Perhaps it was because there was a force in the world that hated good things. So it tried to spoil the beautiful creation the Great Darkness made. It twisted some beings and made them into monsters. There were not as many of them as there were of normal beings, but these monsters were greedy, powerful, and dangerous.

"Luckily," Great-grandmother added, "they are also stupid."

She had told me the names of some of those creatures. It was clear to me which one this was. Mamaskwa. Toad Woman.

"Wheeeere did my food go?" Toad Woman said, shaking her head as she looked around.

I whistled from the top of the tree. "Stupid one," I said, "look up here."

Toad Woman stared up at me. "Hrrrrrmpph," she said in her quavery voice. "You are not good food. Why did I think you a human being? You are a nassssty owl."

Her words made me angry. If I had been a person, one of those helpless little human nestlings that I sometimes watched as they stumbled about on feet even more uncertain than a fledgling's wings, she would have eaten me. As she had probably eaten others.

But even though I was an owl and not the one she had thought to lure to her big mouth, she was still staring at me with hungry eyes. She had also stealthily moved close enough to my side of her pool to grasp with one big hand the tree in which I was perched.

"Commmme heeerrre," she trilled.

I was not about to do that. I jumped up into flight just as Toad Woman yanked the red willow out of the bank and down into the water with her.

"Nasty owl?" I called down to her. "You don't know how nasty I can be."

I flew back to that pile of rocks and picked up the biggest one I could lift. Then I flew back, gaining height as I did so. I hovered carefully over the pond that was far below me, took note of the dark shadow there, and then dropped that heavy rock. Down it fell, down, down, and then . . .

THONK!

"WAAAGGGH. THAT HURT ME."

Good, I thought as I flew back for another rock. *Hrrllll. Get used to it.*

I didn't drop rocks all through the night. I took several breaks to fly off, catch a mouse, a vole, a squirrel, a tangy shrew. But I came back faithfully. That pond of Toad Woman's was not as deep as I had thought it to be. When Toad Woman stood up in the deepest spot, her head was almost out of the water. From above I could always see her, even when she ducked down as far as she could. Not far enough to keep those rocks from hurting when they hit. Eventually I used up all of the rocks in that pile and had to find another one. But there were lots of other piles.

I came back the next night, and the one after that. Owls can be very determined. On the fourth night, though, when I returned to the pond, there was no sign of Toad Woman in its dark waters. However, I did see wide tracks leading off in the direction of the sunset.

I flew to the top of the biggest pine and stared off in that direction. If I followed her trail, I supposed I could find her.

Great-grandmother landed on the limb next to me. I hadn't told her what I had been doing every night, but I realized now that she knew. She had probably been watching the whole time.

"She is gone, Wabi," Great-grandmother hootuled. "You have done enough. The little ones of our village are safe now."

"Our village?" I said. "Don't you mean the little ones of the human beings?"

Great-grandmother turned her head to look in the other direction. She didn't say anything, even though I waited and waited. But then another question came to me.

"Great-grandmother," I said, "why did Toad Woman think I was a human at first? Was it because I spoke human words?"

"Wabi," Great-grandmother said to me, "that is part of the answer. But there is more that I am still not ready to tell yoooou. You must find out for yourself."

CHAPTER 8
People-Watching

DID MY GREAT-GRANDMOTHER MEAN FOR me to spend more time sitting in the cedars at the edge of Great Waterfall Village watching the human beings? Before, I had only gone once in a while to wonder at their curious ways. Now, though, hardly a night—or a day—went by without my spending time there, studying them closely.

I liked watching their little ones in particular. They spent so much of their time in play. We owls do a bit of playing—dropping things in flight and catching them, bouncing up and down on supple branches—but those human little ones were much more inventive. They played alone and with each other and with the four-legged ones that were always following them about.

They made their own little upside-down nests, copying

the ones their elders wove from branches and grasses and big pieces of birch bark. They twisted and wrapped fibers to make strings and then took supple little tree branches to fashion bows and arrows like the elders used. They played a game where they shot at little hoops they rolled across the ground. It looked like fun to me. I enjoyed watching them play it.

So it went day after day as I kept on listening and learning about things that an owl would never use. Such things as clothing. I did pity them for having to wear clothing. The Great Darkness clearly loved owls much more than humans. We owls were given feathers to wear. Our feathers kept us warm in the coldest winds and cool during the times of heat. Humans had to put on leggings and breechclouts, shirts and robes and hats. They even had to cover their tender feet, which were not tough like an owl's, with moccasins. Poor, pathetic things.

Of course, at first, I did not know what clothing was. So it was that, one day in early summer, I saw something that shocked me. I was perched near a place where the river flowed into a calm little pool. It was early morning. Along down the bank came one of those humans, a big male. That human walked right down to the water's edge and then sat down and—wahh-ahhh!—pulled the skin right off his feet. I stared, certain that blood would start flowing. Instead, the human yanked what I thought was all of his skin off the top of his body. I almost fell out of my tree! The skins that this human had been wearing were not his own, but had been taken from other animals.

Now I could see the shape of that human's body, the play

of muscles under the real skin, which was smooth and brown. The man waded into the stream and began to wash.

He was not there long before another human came along, a small one whose clothing (I had now figured out that it was not her skin) was that of a little girl. She called softly to the first one standing knee-deep in the cool water. The man turned and showed his teeth at her.

Is the man threatening the little girl? I wondered. It was the first time I had ever seen a human smile.

But the little girl showed her teeth back at the man. She made friendly sounds as the man finished washing and then came to sit beside her. I listened closely.

"Big Brother Melikigo," she said, throwing twigs at his head, "why are you so lazy? While you've been busy washing your hair, the other men have been cutting trees for the new wigwam."

"Little Sister Dojihla," the man said, "if you are so worried about building that wigwam, why aren't you back there helping them?"

I had not been watching and listening for long before I heard something else. It was the sound of stealthy feet creeping through the brush at the edge of the riverbank, stalking up slowly in preparation for attack.

I turned my head to stare down into the brush. Some think that owls cannot see in the daylight, but that is not so. Our eyes are just so big that too much light is painful. I saw clearly what was getting closer and closer.

It was a gagwanisagwa. It was not the worst or the largest of the non-animal monsters that hunted humans, but it was bad enough. It was not much larger than a big human, but it made up for its size in its bloodthirstiness. Its body was long and snaky, its many teeth sharp. The legs of the gagwanisagwa are short, and it cannot run swiftly for great distances. But it can move very quickly close to its prey. In this case, it would be two foolish humans.

Great-grandmother had once seen a gagwanisagwa slip up on a small herd of elk in the night. Before she could make a warning sound, it was among them, slashing with its teeth. It killed every one of them, drank some of their blood, then left and did not return.

The gagwanisagwa is a coward. If the man had his bow and arrows with him and was alert, this creature would not dare to attack. But now, with no weapons at hand, those two humans were defenseless.

"Unfair, unfair!" I growled to myself.

I flapped my wings and hooted loudly to get the attention of the two humans. They were too busy talking to hear me, but the gagwanisagwa did. The creature turned its black gleaming eyes toward me. It hissed softly and bared its teeth at me. It was not smiling.

"Go away!" it growled.

"WHOOOO-WHOOO-WHOOO," I called again, louder than before.

This time the little girl, Dojihla, looked up. "Why is that owl making so much noise in the daytime?" she said.

Her brother, Melikigo, did not even look my way. "It's just a bird," he said.

"BOOO-LE-WAAA-TIOOOO," I hooted at them. It was the first time I had tried speaking the words of the two-leggeds to anyone other than my great-grandmother. Surely they would understand.

"Did you hear that?" Dojihla asked. "Did it not sound as if that owl said 'Run away from him'?"

Melikigo laughed. "Don't be ridiculous, Dojihla."

I shook my head. Were all humans as stupid as him? How did they survive? How could an adult like Dojihla's big brother behave as heedlessly as a helpless nestling?

Yet it did not make me angry at him. Instead, my anger focused on that creature about to attack some of my humans. *My* humans.

"Krrooo-oooo," I growled. Then I lifted one foot, looked at my claws, and flexed them. *Nice and sharp,* I thought.

The gagwanisagwa was still hidden, but it was now almost close enough to attack. I swooped down over the humans, who did not even look up, banked, and dove, claws held out, into the brush.

I had been aiming at its eyes, but the gagwanisagwa moved its head a little too quickly. All I came away with was the larger part of one of its ears in my right talon.

Ah well, try again.

The gagwanisagwa snarled and struck at me, but I was out of its range with most of its other ear in my left talon and making my next circle to attack. This time I came in from behind, screamed, dove, and ripped a nice big patch of skin off its rump.

In addition to blood, it also drew a yelp from the creature.

"ROWP!" it yipped.

That sound made Dojihla look up again toward the riverbank, where there was now considerable thrashing in the brush as the creature tried in vain to escape me.

"What is that owl doing?" she said.

"Just trying to catch some little bunny," Melikigo replied in a bored voice. "It does not concern us. Let us go back to the village now."

And as I continued my attack, they wandered away, never knowing that I had saved them.

CHAPTER 9
Better to Be an Owl

A NICE COATING OF SNOW had fallen over the land. I liked this season of snow. To me it was another sign of how much the Great Darkness cared for owls. The nights were wonderfully long in this season. And the fact that the nights were long for only this one part of the great circle of seasons made it all the better. If they were always long we might not appreciate them as much. It would be like eating nothing but one kind of mouse all the time.

Although meadow mice certainly were tasty. Urp. I took a breath and then coughed up a nice firm ball of little crunched bones and hair. What a pleasant reminder of a good meal an owl pellet is! I spat it out and heard it fall into the soft snow that had drifted around the roots of the cedar.

"Back where you came from," I hooted softly. "Thank you for feeding me. Now become another mouse."

Speaking our thanks whenever we cough up a pellet is one of our oldest customs.

It was Great-grandmother who taught me the reason.

"The Great Darkness meant for us to always be thankful. The little scampering ones keep us alive by making themselves easy for us to eat. Those little balls of fur and bones that we spit out onto the ground will make more of those little scampering ones for us to eat in the seasons to come. We do not eat their spirits, only their little bodies. We eat them, then we give back their bones. If we did not give thanks, their spirits would go far away where we could not find them. And then we would have no more food. Always remember to give thanks, great-grandson."

It made good sense, and I had noticed that even the human beings expressed their thanks for the food they were given. I'd watched a human hunter do so just the other day after he killed a moose.

But it was so hard for humans to get their food. They didn't just gulp it down whole the way we owls usually did with most of our food. Humans had to spend much effort taking off the skins—not even with their own mouths, but with cutting tools that they struggled to make. Then they had to cut out the meat and gather wood for making fires to burn that good food because their weak little mouths and delicate stomachs could not accept it unless it was cooked. How sad!

The night was almost over. Perhaps there was just time for one more brief hunt. But for some reason I didn't feel like hunting. Instead I wanted to visit the village where my humans were.

They were no longer in the village below the falls. When the season changed, they had moved to another place. They did this every year, moving their little village to be near their food. When they lived below the falls, much of what they ate was fish. But in the season of snow they moved upland to hunt the big animals. Without wings they couldn't go from one place to another as quickly as an owl can. So they moved everything and everyone, leaving the frames of their old nests behind and making new ones in their new village. It was so much harder to be a human than an owl.

By the time I reached Snow Season Village, the light of the Day Fire had returned. I hid myself in a snowy pine to watch. The humans were already awake and their little ones were playing a game I had not seen before. As I had hoped, Dojihla, the little girl I had protected from the gagwanisagwa, was among them.

I liked watching her. Even though she was far from the largest child, she seemed to be their leader. They were sliding down the smooth snow on the hill behind their village. They slid on their bellies like otters. I could hear their shrieks as they did so. I used to think those were sounds of distress, but I had learned that it was their way of laughing. Not as expressive a sound as the little chuckle we owls make, but I liked it.

The more I watched, the more enjoyable their game appeared. Dojihla seemed to delight in both tripping the larger boys and carefully helping the smallest children through the deep snow. I was glad to see that she seemed to be much more watchful than any of the others. One who is always looking and listening is more likely to survive. She even cast her eyes my way, peering suspiciously into the place where I was concealed in the pine. But I was deep in the branches and my white feathers blended in so well that I am sure she could not see me.

Before long some of the bigger humans came out and joined the little ones. Dojihla's big brother was among them, carrying a large, flat piece of bark. By sitting on the bark he could go down the slope almost as fast as if he had wings. Just before he went down the second time, though, Dojihla sneaked up behind him with an armful of snow that she dropped on his head. He laughed and threw snow back at her. The other humans joined in, laughing loudly. The oldest of the humans, those who walked not with two legs but with three, using a stick as another leg, came out of their nests. They were laughing too.

As I watched them, I felt a warmth in my heart that I had not felt before. We owls seldom gather together in a group, and no owl had ever played a game like that. I wished that I could join in. Strangely, instead of being happy, I now felt sad. I could watch no longer.

I took flight from the pine tree, my wings spreading a cloud of snow as I did so. I know that Dojihla heard me. From high above I saw her staring at the cloud of snow still falling from the branch where I had been. But none of the other happy humans noticed. They were playing and laughing and shouting so loudly that they would not even have noticed some great monster coming out of the dark forest to destroy them. Just in case, I made a big circle around the village, but I saw nothing more dangerous than a few panicky white rabbits.

I flew until I came to another hill of snow like the one they had been sliding upon. I landed at the top of the hill and looked around. There was no person or bird or animal anywhere in sight.

How was it that they did it? I leaned forward until my chest was almost touching the snow. Then I leaned farther forward and kicked with my feet. But instead of sliding, I buried myself in the snow. I stood up, shaking the snow out of my beak and eyes.

Foolish, I thought. *Wabi, you are foolish. It is better to be an owl than a human.*

But as I flew back to my roosting place to sleep through the day, I kept thinking of that whole village of humans laughing and playing together. Were we owls really the most favored of all the creatures made by the Great Darkness? Perhaps being a human was almost as good as being an owl.

CHAPTER 10

The Greedy Eater

I FLEW SLOWLY OVER THE meadow below the beaver pond. Sure enough, there he was, making his way through the grass. Just like an owl, he was hunting for mice. Although mice were not the only things he hoped to find. It was the season to dig for grubs, and any unwary cricket or grasshopper would also be fair game.

As he would be for an owl as big as I was. He neither saw nor heard me coming as I swooped down—to land right in front of him. He jumped back, startled. He lifted his tail and stomped his front feet, turning in a half circle to display more clearly the broad white stripe that ran from the top of his head all the way to the end of his fluffy tail.

"I'll shoot, I'll shoot," he chirruped at me. "Watch out! Watch out!"

Much good that would do him against an owl. I almost chuckled, but then remembered why I had been searching for this one.

"Segunk," I hooted softly. "Smelly One. Be calm. Do not use your weapon."

"Why not? Why not?" he chirruped again, stomping his feet a little more softly this time.

"Look at me," I said. "I am an owl. Even if you shoot me with your weapon, it would not bother me. I would still eat you."

This was true and the skunk knew it. We horned owls are the only ones who regularly hunt skunks. Their smell does not bother us at all. We find it rather pleasant. It does not even stick to our feathers. Of all the various creatures great and small, we are the only ones that skunks fear.

Segunk lifted his tail even higher, still threatening me but beginning to look confused. *Why would an owl talk with a creature he intended to eat?* Skunks are not good at thinking. With a weapon such as theirs, thought is seldom necessary.

"No, no," he chirruped, doing a little half circle of a dance. "No, no. If I do not shoot, if I do not shoot, you will eat me, you will eat me."

"No," I said, speaking very simply so that he could understand. "Help me and I will not eat you. Help me and I will never bother you again."

Slowly, Segunk lowered his tail.

The cave's mouth was so well hidden in the tangle of dead tree limbs that it did not seem that large. But I knew that the creature that hid within that cave was not a small one. It had piled those dead branches to conceal its hiding place. I was the only one who knew that it had taken shelter there.

I could smell its thick odor. It was not a sharp stinging smell like Segunk's—a scent that meant life, powerful life. The scent of this creature was different. Even though it was sickeningly sweet, I knew that it meant death.

Why did I know the creature was there? Aside from being able to smell it from a look away? It was because I kept such close watch over my village of human beings. I had been doing this for a dozen turns of the seasons. I had watched their nestlings grow—especially Dojihla. She had grown tall and strong over the past three winters. I liked the way she gathered flowers in the spring and wove them into little circles to place on the heads of the small children. I liked the way she told her older brother and her parents in such great detail about all the things she had done each day. (Having good owl ears and a conveniently thick tree to conceal myself in made it easy for me to listen. And I never fell asleep while she was in the middle of a story, as her brother often did.) Of all the humans, she was the one I most enjoyed watching and listening to. I even enjoyed watching her bully the other children of her own age, telling them what they should or should not do.

At times, I wondered what it was about humans, and this one human girl in particular, that attracted me. Or what it was about me.

I was now a fully mature owl, yet I had no interest in finding another owl as a mate. Instead, whenever I was not hunting or sleeping, I stayed close to the humans, watching and keeping watch.

Which had led me to this new creature. It had come crawling and skulking down from the broken cliffs a few days ago. It looked something like a big human being. But it was not. Its teeth were long and sharp, its hands clawed, its little eyes as yellow as pine pitch. Its elbows and knees bent strangely and it did not walk upright. It was one of those monsters that I had heard the humans tell stories about when they wanted to frighten their little ones into obedience.

"If you do not share your food, you will turn into one of those awful beings. You will become a mojid, a Greedy Eater."

I loved to hide in a nearby tree when human stories were being told. Some of them were fine ones. Others, I must admit, were rather foolish, for they indicated that the Great Darkness—who they called the Great Mystery—liked humans better than all others.

"Not humans!" I hooted out one night in spite of myself when I heard such a silly thing said. "Owls are the favorite ones!"

I had been a little too loud, and the storyteller stopped his words.

"Shall I go out and throw a stick at that owl?" I heard a certain young woman's voice ask the storyteller. I knew that voice: Dojihla, of course. She was just like me in that whenever a story was being told, she was eager to listen. As usual, I enjoyed hearing her talk, despite the rude action she had just suggested.

"No," the old man answered in an amused voice. "When you hear an owl call that way, it is a good thing. It means no enemy is nearby. If there was any danger out there, that owl would be frightened and make a cry of alarm and fly away."

"Gracccck," I muttered, clacking my beak. "That shows how much you know about owls."

I had heard several stories about mojidak. None of them were pleasant. As I watched that Greedy Eater skulk its way down out of the hills, I realized that the stories had been true. It really was unpleasant, disgusting, and dangerous.

Unfortunately, it was also elusive. Somehow it heard that first big rock I dropped and it jumped aside. Too bad. That stone would have split its head open like an egg.

It ran into the cave before I could get back with another rock. I wondered where this mojid came from. Probably from someplace where it had just eaten its whole family. According to the human stories, that is what the mojidak do—they eat each other as readily as they devour almost anything else that moves.

I couldn't go into the cave after it. I made a pile of stones on the top of the cliff and waited patiently. But it was crafty. It refused to come out. Sooner or later, it hoped, I would abandon my vigil and it would be able to make its way close enough to the village. I didn't even want to think about what it might do there.

It was holed up in that cave, but it was not about to starve. Somehow, perhaps when I was off gathering more stones, it had managed to catch some small creature. I had heard something whimpering and then growling in weak but brave defiance from inside that cave. But the mojid had not yet eaten it. Greedy Eaters like to torture and play with their food before they kill it. I decided I could wait no longer. That is why I enlisted Segunk's help.

Segunk looked pleased as he stood in front of the cave

mouth. There is always something self-satisfied about a skunk when it is about to confront a bigger creature that doesn't know what sort of surprise it has coming.

"I go in now?" Segunk chirped, balancing himself on his two front legs and hopping forward. "I go in now?"

"Go," I hooted, nodding my head.

Segunk trotted to the cave mouth, slid through the piled branches, and looked into the darkness.

"Hello," Segunk called out. "Here I am, little creature good to eat. Here I am." He vanished into the cave.

Although I flew up to my pile of rocks to pick a good heavy one, I could still hear what was happening below. Segunk's little feet were picking their way in deeper and deeper. The sound of the Greedy Eater's breathing was growing heavier as it became more excited about a foolish little one actually entering his lair.

Then I heard the mojid's voice.

"I have you!" he snarled.

"Something else, something else I have," Segunk chirruped.

Psssssshhhhhhh!

"AH-GAH, AH-GAH." The sound of the mojid's choking coughs as he tried to escape those stinging fumes echoed loudly.

"AH-GAH, AH-GAH." The mojid came stumbling out of the cave. He rubbed his yellow eyes that were so blinded, he could not see anything. Including my nice heavy stone.

The sound was very satisfying. It was a combination of a thonk and a splat.

I dropped down to land by the creature's body just as

Segunk came strolling out of the cave. Almost all of his spray had been absorbed by the monster, so the little creature that came stumbling out of the cave behind Segunk was sneezing from the smell but wasn't completely blinded.

It was the one I had heard whimpering and growling. I sat there as it came up to me. I suppose I should have flown off, but for some reason I did not understand, I stayed.

It was a wolf cub. It trotted up to me, sneezed one more time, and then looked right into my eyes. Then it whined and licked my beak with its tongue.

Segunk was quietly making his way back down into the meadow. But the wolf cub showed no signs of wanting to go anywhere. It nuzzled me with its nose.

Strange, I thought. Then I leaned forward to preen the hair on the back of its neck with my beak.

CHAPTER 11
A Wolf Cub

DO YOU KNOW HOW MUCH food a wolf cub eats?

Too much, that is how much.

I probably should not have fed him. But he looked so starved that it just seemed like the right thing to do. It was made especially clear when, as I was preening his fur with my beak (now, why did I do that?), he looked up at me and whimpered something in a soft little voice.

Because of that strange gift of understanding that my great-grandmother told me she and I shared, I knew what his whimpers meant.

Malsumsis hungry. Want to eat.

I turned my head around to look back at the dead mojid. The wolf pup—Malsumsis, as he called himself—turned his body to follow my gaze. The mojid's smell had been sickeningly sweet before being struck by Segunk's spray. Malsumsis wrinkled up his nose. Now it was totally disgusting. Not good food at all. I wondered if even the turkey buzzards that were now circling overhead would eat it.

Malsumsis turned back to me. His eyes looked up into mine and he whined again.

Hungry.

Then he leaned against me with his shoulder.

He almost knocked me over. I looked bigger than him and I was certainly much stronger, but owls are not heavy creatures. Our bones are hollow and our feathers, though bulky, are light. That is why we are able to ride the wind as we do. Even though this wolf puppy was half my size and underfed, he was heavier than me.

I hopped back and examined him. His coat, except where I had preened it, was scruffy. Ribs showed along his sides. He had gone without food for longer than the brief time he'd been held in that cave by the Greedy Eater. This was strange. I'd watched wolf packs many times in the past. I always enjoyed the way they played with their little ones, fed them and cared for them. It wasn't just the mothers and fathers of the cubs that took care of them, but all of the adults of their pack.

Then it came to me. It had been a long time since I'd heard the night singing of the wolf pack that ranged the woods above the waterfall. At least two full moons had come and gone. Had this little one belonged to the Upriver Pack?

"Where are your parents? Your pack?"

He lowered his head till his nose touched the ground.

I waited, rocking from side to side, but he said nothing.

Finally, I broke the silence. "Wait here," I hooted. "I'll be back."

It was a good night for hunting. It didn't take long at all for me to come back with a nice fat bunny. It would have been a full night's food for me, but Malsumsis made short work of it, then licked his chops and asked for more.

Two bunnies, six mice, and four voles later, he was finally full... and I was exhausted. The sun would soon rise. It was time for me to rest.

I opened my wings to take flight. I had just enough energy left to fly back to my roosting place on the other side of the valley.

The wolf cub cocked his head as I did so. Somehow, I could read what he was thinking. *Are you coming back?*

I had helped enough. His little belly was as round and taut as one of the drums the humans struck with sticks when they sang and danced. It was time for him to be on his own.

"I am going," I hooted. "Travel well."

I glanced down once as I flapped my wings to gather height. Malsumsis was watching me intently.

Without wings there is no way he can follow me. That is what I assumed as I soared over the treetops, leaving him far behind. I reached my nice hidden roosting place, settled in, and slept soundly all through that day.

What woke me up was not the welcome return of darkness. It was a little voice whimpering from the base of my tree.

Hungry. Want to eat.

Strangely, I was not upset as I looked down. I felt something like pleasure when I saw the wolf cub there, sitting back on his haunches and smiling up. Although he did not have wings, he did have a nose. I should have remembered that no creature has a stronger sense of smell than a wolf. He could have found me even if I had gone four times as far.

I shrugged my shoulders. Then I spread my wings and hopped off the limb. It was going to be a long night.

Luckily for both of us, that season had brought forth more rabbits than usual. As the narrow face of the moon became full, I fed my little friend and he grew. Each day Malsumsis slept faithfully at the foot of my tree and each night I went out in search of food for him. The moon thinned and filled again. Now he was hunting on his own, creeping up and pouncing on mice and voles in the meadow. Soon he'd be catching his own rabbits.

But even once he was able to get most of his food by himself, he did not leave me. Was it because I had saved his life? Or was it that he felt some strange liking for me? Those questions I cannot answer. All I knew was that wherever I flew, the little cub came trotting after me.

Then, one night when I woke, I heard a different sound from below.

Look down here.

I looked. Malsumsis was sitting there proudly, the carcass of a grouse resting at his feet. He had brought food for me.

I dropped down to the ground and plucked feathers from the grouse's chest as I held it firmly with one foot. Malsumsis sat back, watching me accept his gift. I dug my beak in. *Ah, still nice and warm.*

When I was finished, Malsumsis nuzzled me gently and lowered his head. I leaned forward and began to preen his hair.

A large shape came floating down out of the night and landed on a low branch just above us. Malsumsis looked up and growled. Even though he was still just a cub, he was ready to protect me.

"Be calm," I hooted to him in a reassuring voice.

There was no need to worry about the one who had just joined us. It was, of course, my great-grandmother. Now that I was a full-grown owl, I no longer saw her every night. I still went to her whenever I needed guidance. But I had not even thought to ask her what to do about this wolf cub who now believed that he and I belonged to each other.

"Wabi, are you starting your own wolf pack?" Great-grandmother whootuled. I could hear the amusement in her voice.

I might have said no, but I didn't want to hurt the cub's feelings.

"Great-grandmother," I said, "this is Malsumsis. He is my good friend."

I didn't say anything about how I had saved him and then fed him. If I knew my great-grandmother, she'd been somewhere watching me all the time.

"Wabi," she said, chuckling, "do you want to be a human?"

"No!" I said, clacking my beak in annoyance.

What a ridiculous question that was. Why would my grandmother ask it?

She looked down at me and nodded. "Do you know the story the humans tell of how the dog came to them?" she asked.

"Yes," I said.

Just two seasons ago, while hiding in my favorite cedar

near the village, I had overheard Dojihla telling some smaller children that very story.

"Sit down," she had said. "All of you pay attention. Dog was once like the wolf. Then the human beings were created. All the animals were given a choice about how they would live. All the other animals wanted to either go their own ways or treat the humans as prey. They were as foolish as some of the boys in this village who think they are grown-ups even though they are still just silly boys. But not dog. Only dog chose to live with the humans. They promised to always be friends to the people—even those who were as stupid as those boys in our village that I just mentioned, like Wikadegwa and Onegig and Agwegajezid."

After hearing her story, I began to pay more attention to the dogs. It was true. Those dogs seem to be the most loyal creatures in the world. Even when they were treated badly, they still stayed by the humans, guarding them and following them.

Some of those humans—the kinder ones—were very good to their dogs. Dojihla, despite the way she treated the big boys of her village, was one of those who treated her dogs very well. I liked watching the way she played with them, throwing things for them to catch and bring back, wrestling with them. It looked like fun as they romped about. But that did not mean I was envious. By taking care of a wolf cub, I was not acting like a human being raising a dog. Not one bit. I was not trying to imitate the humans.

Why would an owl ever want to be one of those pathetic, featherless beings?

I looked up at the branch. Great-grandmother was gone. I

had been so lost in my thoughts that I had not even noticed her leaving.

Malsumsis nudged me with his nose.

Harruf? he barked.

"Yes," I agreed, nuzzling his neck with my beak before spreading my wings. "Let us go hunting."

CHAPTER 12
Miserable

I WAS MISERABLE. I HAD never felt so unhappy or confused.

I sat on the branch of the cedar tree, peering out through its thick, protecting boughs that hid me from sight. My second eyelid was closed against the light of the sun. I have not mentioned it before, but that is yet another way that the Great Darkness made us owls better than human beings. We owls were given two eyelids for each eye. That second inner eyelid, which is filmy, can be closed to clean our eyes or protect them from getting hurt. It also cuts down the brightness of day when an owl cannot sleep at the normal time.

But I was more than watchful. I was ill at ease, confused, upset, and several other things I could not find words for. I felt as if I were being spun about by a whirlwind. What was happening to me?

Malsumsis sensed my disquiet. We had been hunting together with the usual success. Seasons had passed since he was a small starved pup, and my friend had grown into a huge wolf, bigger than any I had ever seen before. Even after he was grown, Malsumsis had stayed with me, as loyal as he would have been to his own pack that had disappeared. It was strange the way they had vanished. There was no sign of them anywhere in our valley. The last time he had seen his pack was when he fell into the river as a puppy and was washed by the swift current downstream, where the long, hard hands that pulled him out had been those of the mojid.

Each time we hunted, we also looked for signs of Malsumsis's family, but with no luck. What we did find in the way of family was more of my own. My sister had been staying in the far end of our valley, well away from my hunting grounds.

One night I was flying high, the soft warm wind under my wings, looking out across the night land that spread beneath me. I looked in the direction where the sun always disappeared below the horizon. First there was the forest stretching beyond in a carpet of dark green. Then there was the blue mountain and the hills circling around it like bear cubs following their mother.

Beyond that mountain were even higher mountains, and beyond them? I did not know. Once an owl has found his or her own hunting ground, that is where he stays. I knew, from having heard the humans talk, that there were other human villages off in the winter land direction, the summer land direction, and in the direction of the dawn. There were stories about those places. Some humans went there often. But none of the humans seemed to know anything about what lay beyond the night mountains. No one ever went that way. In the past, no one who dared to travel over those mountains had ever come back.

What was to be found there? I wondered as I gazed. Had Malsumsis's pack gone there? Were there other creatures even more dangerous than the mojid and the gagwanisagwa and Toad Woman? Were there other owls there?

Then, to my surprise, I heard something below me. It was another owl. It was not calling from some faraway valley but from the edge of my own hunting grounds. What nerve! I glided down to take a look. A fat male owl, perhaps half my size, was sitting on one of my perches on the overhanging limb of a big hemlock tree.

I landed quietly behind him. Not only was this fat little owl too stupid to stay in his own home ground, he was also not even watchful enough to have seen me land. He was so much smaller than me that I didn't feel the need to do anything more to get rid of him than say a few well-chosen words.

"You are on my branch," I said.

The fat little owl swiveled his head so fast to look at me that he almost fell.

"Who?" he said, edging quickly away from me toward the end of the branch, which began to bend under his weight. "Who are you?" There was terror in his voice as he stared up at me.

But I didn't answer him right away. Though many seasons had passed, I recognized that voice of his even if he didn't recognize mine. It was my bullying big brother. *He* was the one who grew up to be a runt!

"Who-o-o?" he said again in a trembling voice. He was

so far out on the end of the limb that he was almost upside down.

"Move!" I hooted loudly. That was all he needed to hear. He flopped awkwardly off the branch, and almost landed on Malsumsis's head. My wolf friend had been waiting at the bottom of the tree and watching. He woofed at my brother, who managed to finally get his wings spread and flap away in panic.

It was hardly a victory for me. He was so pathetic. I shook my head now, remembering. The memory suited my foul mood. I noticed a hare, dropped down to the ground to grab it, and carried it over to Malsumsis. I didn't tear off a single piece of meat, even though Malsumsis waited patiently, as always, for me to start feeding first.

"Whoo-ah-whooo," I hooted halfheartedly. "Eat it all."

Malsumsis did as I said. A few gulps and the entire hare was gone. Then he looked at me and whined.

What's wrong?

"Nothing," I said.

He nuzzled me with his nose. I didn't respond. He jumped back, whimpered, flattened himself on his stomach as he crawled toward me. Then he rolled over onto his back and let his tongue loll out. Very funny. It didn't cheer me up.

I tilted my head to look up at the sky. It was starting to show signs of dawn. Soon the humans would come out of their upside-down nests to go down to the river and bathe.

"I have to go," I said to Malsumsis.

I jumped up into flight and he did not follow me. He saw where I was headed. He usually did not accompany me when I went to watch the human beings. Their dogs did not like his scent and would complain loudly, drawing the attention of the humans to him.

It was not that Malsumsis was afraid of humans and their dogs. He could easily beat any dog, even a pack of them, and I doubted that any human was a good enough shot to hit my friend with a bow and arrows. Not only had he grown to be the largest wolf I had ever seen, he was also the fastest and most agile. But he knew that I liked to watch those human beings without disturbing them or calling any attention to myself.

And so I watched and waited, feeling worse and worse. The pain in my gut was like being impaled on the sharp end of a broken branch. I sat there hoping that when I coughed up my next pellet of fur and bunny bones, the pain would come up with it, tumble to the ground with a soft thump and be gone.

Urp. Cough. Spit.

No such luck. Pellet ejected, pain still present.

Then, at last, Dojihla walked by. She was wearing her white doeskin dress decorated with porcupine quills that had been sewn on to make a pattern of leaves and flowers. As soon as I saw her, my pain went away. I felt happy just watching her walk past.

And suddenly it came to me. I understood what it was that I was feeling. It explained so much. Such as why, during the cold moons of the last winter, I hadn't been one of those male owls filling the night with hopeful burbles and hoots, just waiting for the higher pitched voice of an interested female owl to answer me.

I looked at Dojihla and realized that I had fallen in love with her. That was it! I felt like singing one of those sweet little owl love songs that thrills your chosen one right down to the pinfeathers. I wanted to share a branch with her and lean my head against her.

Then it hit me like a great gust of sleet-filled wind. I would never find Dojihla sitting on a branch beside me. She was a human, not an owl. I was in love, but there was nothing I could do about it.

CHAPTER 13

She Goes By

DAYS AND NIGHTS HAD PASSED since I realized that I was in love. How many? I don't know. All I knew was that I was happy when I could see her and miserable when I couldn't. I had worn all the bark off the tree limb by impatiently rocking back and forth.

Where is she? Ah, here she comes.

I sat in the tree and cooed softly to myself as Dojihla passed. Naturally she didn't see me. Dojihla. Isn't it a beautiful name? It is almost a song. Dojihla, Dojihla. And it is perfect for her. It means "She goes by." Which is what she did whenever I saw her. She just went by, not noticing me hidden in the cedar tree.

And what if she had looked up? All she would have seen was an owl. Admittedly, a very large, extremely capable young male owl. She would surely have taken note of the fact that he was an owl well above average. No way could she miss that special gleam of intelligence in the eyes, the sensitivity of the beak, the way each feather had been so elegantly preened. All right, I know. I was dreaming.

These days, to be honest, most of the dreaming I did was daydreaming. I was not sleeping the way I should. I was spending so much of my time awake during the day that I was actually dozing off at night. If it hadn't been for the hunting that Malsumsis did and his insistence that I always take the first bite of whatever he caught, I probably would have been losing weight. But just having the chance to watch Dojihla made my sleepless days worth while.

It wasn't a sudden thing. My feelings for her had grown over the years the way a sapling grows with the passage of seasons until one day you realize that a tall tree is standing where once there was just an open place in the forest. It had begun with watching the children play, back when she was one of them, and wishing that I could join in. I had grown used to the way she talked, the way she laughed, the way she was always the first to ask questions . . . the way she bullied the other boys and girls.

Season after season, Dojihla had always been the leader in whatever mischief they all got into. She had been the first to try to walk on the thin ice on the ponds, the first to climb to the top of the tallest tree. (She even decided once to climb the very tree I was in. I had to scuttle to the far side, hunch down, sit very still, and pretend to be the broken stub of a branch.)

Dojihla! She was the one who led the other children on

hunting expeditions with their small bows and arrows. She even dared, with the bravest of the other young ones, to venture into a certain swamp where it was rumored that a child-eating monster lurked. (Of course, you know that was not true—at least not after I got through with Toad Woman.)

One of Dojihla's favorite games was going out with a group of boys and girls to search for someone they called the Village Guardian.

"The Village Guardian," she would say to whatever group of children she had managed to gather to listen to her opinions, "is a tall, strong, handsome man. He roams the woods by himself, protecting the people from any danger that might threaten our village, such as monsters."

"Are there really monsters?" some small child might ask.

"Oh, yes," Dojihla would say, nodding her head wisely. "They are as real as our Village Guardian himself."

That amused me. I knew that there was certainly no such human as the Village Guardian. If there were, I would have seen him while I patrolled around the village each night.

But Dojihla was determined. In fact, when she was younger, she used to lead the other children on expeditions to find him. They would convince this noble but shy person to come and live in the village with everyone else.

"This time," Dojihla would say, as she outlined a plan to climb a steep cliff, "we will surely find the Guardian's hiding place."

It was hard not to chuckle at her insistence that this imaginary being really existed. Especially when she and her hapless band would fail to find any evidence of her mythical hero and she would look at the dirty scratched faces of her troop, and say—to their dismay—"I have a better idea. Now we'll search the blackberry thicket!"

Even the bigger boys never tried to contradict her. If they did, they found themselves on the ground with Dojihla sitting on their chest and making them eat grass.

Of course now that Dojihla was a young woman, she no longer wrestled with the boys. That was not through any choice of her own. She didn't seem to be afraid of anyone or anything. When a certain gleam came into her eye, it meant "Move out of my way or I will *move* you out of my way." Isn't that wonderful? But now, more often than not, the boys she had played with either acted bashful around her or stared when they thought she wasn't looking. (They were extremely careful to not be caught staring. The last young man Dojihla had noticed gaping at her was hit in the face by a fistful of river mud.)

Several seasons had now passed since Dojihla had led a group of other young ones on one of her quests. Her parents were relieved about that. I knew this for a fact, having listened to their conversations about their daughter. They used to worry that she would be hurt during one of those foolhardy expeditions, but they never told her not to go. Now, though, they had the opposite worry. They were afraid that she would never go.

I watched them from my favorite hiding place in the cedar.

"My wife," Dojihla's father said, shaking his head, "it is now two winters since our son, Melikigo, married and went off to the village of his new wife's family. We need a young man to take his place. Our daughter needs to finally take a husband."

"My husband, Wowadam," Dojihla's mother said, "you are right. But I fear our daughter will never have a family of her own. She is so stubborn, and so critical."

"Do you think she will approve of the young man who is coming today?" Wowadam asked.

"What do you think?" Dojihla's mother replied.

Dojihla's father shook his head again and sighed.

I saw their point. Love might have made me sick to my stomach, but it hadn't made me blind. Graceful as Dojihla was, beautiful as she was, perfect as she was in form and movement, that human girl was just as finicky. I knew because I had been watching her so closely—as had every human youth in every nearby village. They all knew Dojihla. She was the lovely maiden with the sparkling eyes and the sarcastic voice—the one whose words were sharper than flint-tipped arrows.

It had gotten to the point where suitors had almost stopped coming around. Most of them had become afraid of what she would say to any man foolhardy enough to seek her hand. With a few well-aimed words or a single gesture she could destroy the tallest, strongest, most capable suitor. However, there always seemed to be at least one who thought he could succeed where others failed.

I flew off to take a look at the new suitor and found him walking along the river on his way to the village. His name, I soon learned—for he had the nervous habit of talking to himself—was Bitahlo.

"I, Bitahlo," he said, as he walked along, "will be the one to win her heart. I am sure of it. My song will show her how I feel. She will not be able to resist its power."

Then he began to sing it. It spoke of Dojihla's beauty and grace. He was right about that. But when he came to the part about her *sweetness,* comparing her to flowers, swaying reeds, and a doe with her fawn, I shook my head with pleasure. I thought I knew how Dojihla would react to that.

I flew back on silent wings and managed to conceal myself in the tree before Bitahlo arrived and stood in front of his prospective bride and her parents.

"I have made this song for you," he announced. Then he sang it.

Dojihla's parents looked over anxiously at their daughter when Bitahlo finished. I was anxious too as I watched from my perch in the cedar. The song had actually not been that bad. Also, to be honest, Bitahlo's voice was good. What if that song actually did work?

Dojihla looked up. Her eyes seemed far away, as if entranced by the song. Bitahlo leaned forward, eager to hear her acceptance of his declaration of love.

"What *was* that?" Dojihla said. "Did I just hear a moose breaking wind?"

I almost fell off my branch with laughter. For his part, Bitahlo went pale, turned, and stalked off.

Dojihla's mother looked up into my tree. "My husband, what is wrong with that owl?" she said. "It sounds as if it is choking."

"Forget the bird, my wife," said Dojihla's father. There was a look in his eyes that told me what had happened was like that last stick pulled from the beaver dam, the one that makes the pent-up water come rushing forth. "We must talk."

Then the two of them went into their lodge where their daughter could not hear them.

Of course I could. If you can hear the deliciously terrified heartbeat of a mouse hiding in the grass far below your treetop perch, it is not at all difficult to make out a human conversation within a nearby wigwam. That conversation! It both worried me and gave me hope.

"Our daughter now has nineteen winters," Dojihla's father whispered. "It is well past the season for her to choose a husband."

"But how can we find any man who is stupid—I mean suitable enough?" said Dojihla's mother. "Our daughter is so choosy."

"My wife," Dojihla's father replied, "we shall no longer allow her to choose. We will have a contest in the old way. The man who brings in the most game in a day will be the winner. Our daughter will have to marry that man. It is an ancient tradition. Even Dojihla cannot refuse to follow it."

I took flight from the tree while they were still talking. I should have been depressed at the thought that Dojihla was going to be forced to take a husband. But I was not. An idea had come to me. It was a crazy idea. It was so strange that I was not sure where it had come from. Still, it made me feel a glimmer of hope. Was it possible? There was only one who could tell me. I had to find my great-grandmother.

CHAPTER 14

One More Question

IN SOME OF HER STORIES, Great-grandmother told that long ago there was not as much distance between the various beings in creation. Back then, things were not as set in their ways as they are now. Nowadays, it seems, if you are a fox, for example, that is what you will always be. But back then you could sometimes become something else. That fox might be able to turn into some other creature.

The thought of one creature turning into another made sense to me. After all, I saw it happen every day, firsthand. There's a nice fat mouse scampering about in the grass. Swoop, grab, gulp. And now that mouse is a mouse no longer, but part of an owl.

But that old way of one thing becoming another did not involve either dying or digestion. It was just plain and simple shape-shifting. In certain of the stories Great-grandmother told me, it happened because some being made a foolish wish. Like the owl who wished it would never grow old and die. The Great Darkness gave that owl its wish, but not as it expected. It was turned into an owl-shaped stone that would never grow old and die. Great-grandmother had pointed that very stone out to me, where it stood at the edge of the chestnut forest.

In other stories, though, the being that changed shapes did so because it had fallen in love with some creature that was of a different kind. Like an owl falling in love with a human.

It took me some looking about, but I finally found my great-grandmother. Instead of her usual perch, she was in a big oak tree near the spot where I had been a nestling.

As soon as I landed silently by her side, she turned her head to look at me.

"Wabi," she said, "you have a question for me."

Not just any question, I thought. This one had been spinning about in my head like a whirlpool. It was the most important question I had ever thought to ask.

"Great-grandmother, was my father a human being who turned into an owl?" I had thought she might hesitate, but to my distress, she did not. Her answer was as quick and simple as it was disappointing.

"Nooooo," she hooted, "he was never anything but an owl."

"Ohhh," I said, lowering my head in dejection.

My thought had been that if my father had turned himself into an owl, perhaps the ability to turn into a human being would be in me.

"Listen to me, Wabi," Great-grandmother hootuled. "Your father was very brave. I never told you, but he gave his life to save me before you were hatched. One night, after I had been hunting very late, I did not choose a good place to hide for the day. A mob of giant crows found me. They would have killed me had not your father flown in and attacked them. He led them away and was never seen again."

I lifted my head up. The story of my father's sacrifice made me feel both proud and sad.

"Why did you wait so long to tell me?" I asked.

Great-grandmother dipped her head. "Because of me, you never knew your father," she said. "I did not want you to hate me."

I rubbed my head against my great-grandmother's shoulder. "I could never hate you," I said in a soft voice. Then I sighed. "I just thought that if my father had been a human, that might explain why I have always been so attracted to them."

"Nooo," Great-grandmother said. "My brave grandson was always an owl. It was your mother who was once a human."

I almost fell off the branch. My beak gaped wide in amazement.

Great-grandmother nodded at me. "It is not a long story, Wabi. Your mother did not like being a human. She did not like all the things she had to do, such things as cooking and skinning deer and making clothes. She wanted to be an owl so that she would never have to do those things again. Long ago, someone else in her family had made such a change, so it was in her to do this. So she went to the place in the forest where the old stories said such things could happen. It was the place where seven stones made a great circle near the foot of a giant oak tree. And she became an owl, leaving behind all that was human."

Great-grandmother chuckled. "Your mother is a beautiful owl, but she has never been very good at being an owl. If your father had not taken pity on her, she would have starved. And after he was gone, when she had you little ones to care for, I stayed close by. Most of the mice she fed you were ones that I caught for her."

My head was truly spinning now. I finally understood why my lazy mother had done such an awful job of caring for me when I was young, why she had not even tried to find me after I fell from our nest. Perhaps it even explained why, after my brother and sister had also left the nest, our mother just disappeared. Being an owl had turned out to be harder than she had expected. Had my mother found some way of going back to being a human again? But that was not what I needed to ask now.

"Great-grandmother," I said. "I have one more question."

My great-grandmother looked off into the forest before she turned her head back to me.

"I am sure that you dooo," she said.

CHAPTER 15
Seven Stones

"AH," GREAT-GRANDMOTHER SAID. THEN SHE sat silently for a long time after I had asked that one more question. It was this:

How can I change into a human being?

I could tell how much my question troubled her. Her eyes were closed and her ear tufts were lowered back on her head. Finally she clacked her beak, opened her eyes, and swiveled her head to look straight at me. Then she made one of those soft little whoot-a-luls that is an owl's way of sighing.

"So-oo-ooo, you are sure this is what you want?"

"Yes."

She sighed again. "Look down."

I looked down over my right shoulder. Malsumsis, who had followed his nose to find me, was sitting there on his haunches at the base of another big oak tree a few steps away from the one in which we sat, looking up expectantly at us. It seemed that Malsumsis could sense that something out of the ordinary was happening—even more out of the ordinary than a wolf having an owl as his best friend.

"Not there, Wabi," Great-grandmother said. "Look to the other side. Right below."

I turned my head to peer over my left shoulder. It took me a moment to realize what I was seeing. There, right below us, were seven tall standing stones. Why had I never noticed them before? They stood as straight as seven giant owls. The way they were arranged in a perfect circle made it seem as if someone had placed them there. In the middle of their circle was a mound of earth that was about the size and shape of a human being lying on its back.

"Long agooo," Great-grandmother said, "there were seven beings. Some said they were owls, for they were as wise as owls. But whatever they were, they could answer any question. They were mdawelinnok, wise ones. But so many came to ask them questions that they grew tired. So they decided to hide. They flew to a place deep in the forest and changed themselves into a circle of seven cedar trees. For a time they were left in peace. But they did not stay silent. They would whisper to each other in the wind, sharing all the things they knew. So it was that someone heard them and told others. Once again, many came to them to ask questions, and because they were trees and rooted to the ground, they could not escape. So one night, they changed themselves back into owls and flew away. They flew to the base of a great tree and there they changed themselves into seven stones. Because they were stones, they remained silent and so it was hard for anyone to find them. But within their circle is the answer to many questions."

I stared down at that circle of stones. The answer to my question had to be there. But what was I supposed to do now?

"Should I fly down there?" I asked.

"No. Stay where you are. First I must ask you, are you certain this is what you want to dooo?"

I nodded my head so hard that I shook loose a few feathers. "Yes!"

Once again, Great-grandmother was silent for a long while. Finally she turned her head one way and then the next, moving her gaze through the circle of creation surrounding us. As she did so, I could see just how old she was, how many seasons of flight were beneath her wings. Lately I had been worried about what would happen when she no longer was able to fly. What if a flock of crows should ever spy her daylight roosting place and then dive in to attack her? Was it wrong of me to want to leave her? For a moment I felt uncertain about the decision I had just made.

I opened my beak, but Great-grandmother raised her wing, gesturing me to stay silent.

"Wabi," she hooted softly, "it is all right. You must do what you must do. Just remember, you will always be yoooo."

Then she took flight.

"Whooo," she said as she circled me the first time.

"Whooo," she repeated as she came around me the second time. I had to keep turning my head to watch her as she flew. I couldn't help it.

"WHOOOOO," she called yet again, flying around me a third time, so fast that I found myself becoming dizzy.

"WHOOO ARE YOOOOOOO?" she hooted so loudly that it almost deafened me as she made a fourth and final tighter circle that ended with her not going around me but flying right at me!

Thoomph! Her right wing struck me in the chest. She didn't hit me hard, but I lost my balance and felt myself falling backward. I tried to open my own wings to catch the wind, but something was wrong. My feathers weren't spreading out as they should. Then, all of a sudden—WHOMP!—I landed on my back right on that mound of earth in the middle of the seven stones. I wasn't hurt, but it took the wind out of me and I didn't feel like moving for a while.

How strange, I thought. *Why wasn't I able to fly?*

Then something even stranger happened. The ground around me began to move and shift. It felt as if I had landed on an ant hill whose occupants had just wakened and were now crawling all over me. I began to sink into the ground. I tried to open my beak to say something, but my mouth was filled with the flow of that glowing earth that was now all around me and all over me. A bright light began pulsing, blinding my eyes to the comforting darkness. Then I became lost in that light.

CHAPTER 16

In the Light of Day

When I opened my eyes again, it was no longer night. I was flat on my back and the bright sun was shining down on me through the leaves. Things looked different. It was as if I was seeing the light in a different way. I tried to close my inner eyelid, but nothing happened.

I wasn't in pain, but when I turned my head, my neck felt unusually tight. I raised my wing to my beak and was shocked at how soft it was. What were these even softer things under it and around my mouth? Lips. I had lips. For that matter, what were these wiggly worms at the ends of my wings? Fingers?

I started to sit up, but was pushed back by two big paws that pressed down on my chest. A large head thrust itself into view, mouth open, long, sharp teeth exposed.

Then a tongue came out and lapped my face.

Are you you? Malsumsis whined.

I lifted my legs, as an owl would do, and pushed against my wolf friend with my feet.

"Get off me," I said.

My voice sounded strange, but it seemed to please Malsumsis. He leaped back, crouched down wagging his tail, ran in a quick circle, picked up a stick and dropped it at my feet. It was his signal to play the game where I would pick up a stick, fly some distance, and drop it. When he had found it and brought it back to me, I would do it again.

I pulled myself up. It was not easy, for it seemed as if the earth itself was sticking to me. Malsumsis sat on his haunches waiting impatiently for me to begin our game.

Oh, all right.

But when I tried to grab the stick in the talons of my right foot, I couldn't do so. No talons. My foot was so stiff. It was just about useless. Without thinking, I reached out with one wing—which was no longer a wing—and grabbed the stick in my what? My hand? Then I drew my wing—er, arm—back and threw the stick as I had seen humans do. To my surprise, the stick went flying far off into the brush. Malsumsis bounded after it.

I looked at myself. My whole body was bare. Not a feather to be seen anywhere. It was not a cold day, but it made me feel exposed everywhere except on my head. There I had long black hair that fell down over my face when I leaned foward. I brushed that hair back with my hand. I truly was a human being.

"Well done, Wabi," said a familiar voice from a low branch just above me.

"Great thanks to you, Great-grandmother," I said. "But..."

I paused. It wasn't because I didn't know what to say, but because I didn't know which to say of the many things that swarmed through my head like bees.

"Great-grandmother," I said, holding up my hands, "what shall I do now? I have no clothing, and humans always wear clothing. And I do not have human weapons to hunt with, and I..."

I stopped, realizing that I was talking far too much. Apparently finding it hard to keep my beak shut was as much a part of my being a human person as it had been when I was an owl.

Great-grandmother nodded her head and lifted up one foot to point with a long talon at a hollow in the base of her tree.

I stood up and walked. Human legs were longer than I had realized, but I got the hang of it quickly. Although they were not useful for grasping things, these human feet were well designed to carry my weight. In no time at all, even faster than I could have hopped as an owl, I reached that hollow and looked inside. My new eyes did not seem to be as good at penetrating the darkness, but there was something in there. I lifted my arms and reached in. My hands proved as good at grasping as my feet had been when I was an owl. I pulled out a long bundle wrapped in deerskin and tied tightly with rawhide.

I put it down on the ground and knelt. And that was extremely weird. Instead of bending backward as legs are supposed to do, my human legs bent forward. I stood and knelt several more times, getting used to the feeling. Then I turned to the bundle again. Those new fingers of mine seemed clever enough to know what to do on their own. Without my telling them, they loosened the rawhide string and unwrapped the bundle.

By now, Malsumsis had returned, a grin on his face and the stick in his mouth. But he dropped it when he saw what I was doing and trotted up to look over my shoulder.

"Hoo-hoo-hoooo," I said in pleasure as my wolf friend and I looked down at what I had revealed.

There were all the clothes a human man would wear, from the fringed shirt and breechcloth down to moccasins that were, I was pleased to see, decorated with porcupine quill patterns much like those on Dojihla's dress.

It was a bit awkward, but with Great-grandmother's hooted instructions to help me, I got the clothing on. Malsumsis was no help at all. He kept picking up pieces of clothing, running about with them, dropping them, and then waiting for me to come get them. He grabbed one of the moccasins in his mouth, dancing close and then leaping away. There was nothing I could do but chase after him to get it back. I dove at him, grabbed him with my new arms. The two of us went rolling around on the ground, just as I had seen human children do with their puppies.

I enjoyed it, but this was no time for play. I had things to do. I pried the moccasin out of his jaws, stood and brushed leaves and dirt from my new clothing. Malsumsis crouched down again, lowering his head to the ground in anticipation of another round of wrestling. I was tempted. I had never been able to do this when I was an owl, and it was such fun. But I shook my head and raised one arm to point at the forest.

"No, my friend," I said in a firm voice. "We will play later. Now go and leave me alone for a while."

Without a whimper of complaint, Malsumsis turned and trotted off into the woods.

I put on the last of the clothing and secured it with its rawhide strings. I held out my arms to show off my clothing, turned around twice, and then looked up at Great-grandmother.

She nodded. "Good, Wabi," she said.

But there was a far-off look in her eyes as she spoke that made me step closer to her.

"Whose clothes were these?" I asked.

Great-grandmother did not answer. She turned her head away from me and looked toward the place where I had landed in the middle of the circle of stones. I followed her gaze. To my surprise, the human-shaped mound had sunk down and was now a depression in the earth. Right where I had been. That was why I had such a hard time sitting up. I'd been half buried in the earth. No, that wasn't exactly it. I'd felt for a moment as if I was part of that earth, and I'd been right. Had I absorbed that whole mound of earth when my body changed shape? I felt my legs and arms with my hands. I felt like flesh, not earth, but it made sense to me. How else could I have become so large? After all, even the biggest owl is much, much smaller and lighter than a human being.

I looked back at my great-grandmother. It was not easy to do. My neck was so stiff! I could just barely turn it from side to side, rather than being able to turn it way around as an owl can.

"Wabi," Great-grandmother said, "do not try so hard to

turn your neck. Human necks are stiffer than an owl's. But your eyes can move farther on their own."

That was true, disconcertingly so. My eyes were not acting properly. Instead of moving with my head, they seemed able to float around on their own. Up and down. Back and forth. It made me dizzy. I closed my eyes tightly. Finally, cautiously, I opened them again, trying to keep careful control of them. Turning both my head and my new, wobbly eyes, I looked once more at the deep, man-shaped indentation in the earth where I had lain.

"My great-grandfather?" I said.

"Hoo-hooo," Great-grandmother replied, bobbing her head. "You have taken back what your great-grandfather left behind."

"Then my mother was not the first in our family to change shape? My great-grandfather too was a human who changed?"

It may seem silly that I spoke it as a question, but there was so much going through my mind at that moment. On the one wing, I had never been more confused. On the other I felt as if I knew and understood more than I had ever known and understood before.

"His human name was Nadialid. He who hunts," Great-grandmother hooted in a voice that was both sad and proud. "But I will not tell you his story today. It is *your* time, great-grandson."

"But I have more questions," I said. "There are more things I must know. Will I always stay a human now? Can I ever change back into an owl again?"

It was strange how speaking with human lips made words

flow so quickly. I had always asked lots of questions, but now I had twice as many to ask and it seemed that I could ask them twice as fast.

Great-grandmother looked amused. "You are who you are," she said. "It will be your choice, great-grandson. Who you really are will never change. Feel your ears."

I reached up. To my surprise, the tops of my ears were long and feathery. They stuck up out of my thick black hair just as the two tufts on top of my head had done when I was an owl.

"Oh no," I moaned. "Now anyone who sees me will know I am different."

My new ears felt pleasant to the touch, but they were a major problem. If I looked in any way like an owl, the humans would not accept me. They might even suspect me of being a monster in disguise.

"Grandmother," I pleaded, "this is serious. I have to hide these."

"Are you sure you want to cover your lovely ears?"

"Yes," I said. "I am very sure. Tell me what I can do."

Grandmother did not reply. Instead she just lifted her foot and pointed with her claw at the leather headband that still remained on the ground. I had seen such headbands worn by the men of Dojihla's village. I understood. I picked up the leather and wrapped it tightly around my head. Now my owl's ears were pressed down and concealed by the headband. Now I looked like a proper human being.

CHAPTER 17
Hello, My Friends

THERE ARE MANY GOOD REASONS to listen to stories. That day I learned yet another one. If you have heard many stories told to you, it is easy for you to make up new ones to tell to others.

I sat next to the fire looking around the circle of smiling people. Well, not all of them were smiling. Some of the young men who clearly prided themselves on being the best hunters in their respective villages no longer looked so sure of themselves. They did not look so self-satisfied as they had been before I walked into the circle of light cast by the campfire that burns each night in the center of Wolhanadanak.

Wolhanadanak, Valley Village. That is the name Dojihla and her people call this little town where they live. I learned that and any number of things I had never taken notice of before by listening, listening in a different way.

Just as my eyes were not the same as when I had been an owl, so too were my ears changed. Unlike my owl ears, these human ones were set exactly opposite each other on my head. An owl's ears are placed in a better way, one a little higher than the other. That way it is easier to take a bearing on some hidden tasty little thing rustling in the leaves and burrowing under the snow. As a human I also no longer had a nice movable funnel of feathers around each ear that I could arrange in such a way as to bring any sound to me more effectively.

Luckily, though they were stiff and awkward, these new ears were fairly perceptive. (Much better, I would learn, than those of humans who had not begun their lives as owls.) And by tilting my head to one side or the other and cupping my wingtips—hands, I mean—around one ear or the other, I could focus in on sounds with some effectiveness.

I had been listening and watching from the shadows for some time before making my own entrance. I listened more carefully than I had ever listened before as one young hunter after another arrived at the village, introduced himself, and said pretty much the same thing.

"I have come to win the great contest that will begin tomorrow as soon as Kisos, the great sun, shows his face at the edge of the sky."

First, though, each new arrival would call out a greeting before he came into sight.

"Kwai kwai, nidobak!" *Hello, my friends.*

I noticed how many of those young men arrived with their proud mothers close behind them. Nudging them along, in fact. In one or two cases, it seemed as if their sons were not eager to take part in this contest for Dojihla.

"Kwai kwai, nidoba." *Hello, my friend.*

That is the response that would come back to them from the tall gray-haired man who seemed to have the role of welcoming the visitors. That older man stood with his back to the fire, looking down the dark path where each new arrival appeared.

"Bidhabi," the man would then say in a voice almost as deep and pleasant as that of an owl. *Enter and sit.*

I had listened to humans many times, but never before had I been in a situation where I would actually be talking back to them. I needed to know what to say and how to say it. I needed to observe how a proper human behaved in such circumstances. I needed to avoid behaving in a way that would make people suspicious. Most of all, I needed to learn what had to be done to impress Dojihla.

Unfortunately, none of the young men who arrived ahead of me could offer any guidance at all as far as that last thing went. No matter how they carried themselves, no matter how they were dressed, no matter what they said, Dojihla looked at each of them the way a hunter might eye a badly made arrow that he knows will never fly straight.

I had noticed how all the hopeful young men introduced themselves. When they said who their people were and what they were called, familiar places and names often received nods and sighs of approval from the people of her village. But never from Dojihla. She looked as if she had eaten something that was beginning to disagree with her.

None of the men had brought a gift for Dojihla. I looked at the lovely fat mouse I held cupped in my hand. It wiggled its nose and looked back up at me. Of course I hadn't killed it. It is much more polite among owls for your present to still be alive. Then the recipient can enjoy the delicious pleasure of breaking its little neck.

I shook my head. Perhaps not a good idea? Human tastes were different from owls. Come to think of it, I had never seen a human being eat a mouse. My only uncertainty before had been whether to dangle my little squirming token of affection from my hand or my mouth before passing it to the object of my affection. Now I realized how bad an idea that was. Apparently human suitors fed each other such tidbits as live food only when they were inside their upside-down nests. Not out in full view of everyone else.

I went down on one knee and opened my hand.

"Go and make more of your kind so we owls will always have plenty to eat in the nights to come," I whispered to the mouse. It hopped off my hand and dug into the leaves, making so much noise that I was shocked none of the humans seemed to notice.

I should probably go into the village now, I thought.

But still I hesitated, listening. Soon I was glad that I had listened further. What I heard gave me hope.

Dojihla's father had drawn his daughter off to the side and was speaking to her in a voice meant for no one else to hear.

"My daughter," he was saying, "you must accept this. I am sorry that none of these young men interest you. Your dream of marrying the Village Guardian is a foolish one. He is nothing more than a story."

None of those young men interested her? Wonderful! It was clearly the moment for me to make my entrance. I stood up, walked to the edge of their circle of light, and spoke in a clear and pleasant voice.

“KWAI KWAI, NIDOBAK.”

In my excitement, my voice boomed out a bit more than I had intended. Everyone, with the exception of Dojihla, leaped so high at the sound of my friendly greeting that it seemed as if the entire village was trying to find wings and take flight. Dojihla, though, just narrowed her eyes and peered in my direction. Was it eagerness to see who this new arrival was or just annoyance at yet another troubling suitor? I hoped for the former, but my heart sank a bit as I realized it was more likely the latter.

But if you don’t hop off the branch, you’ll never catch anything.

“Kwai kwai, nidobak,” I said again, trying to make my voice as sweet and melodious as possible. And not as loud.

Then I stepped forward to show myself to all those waiting. Nervous eyes were straining in the direction of my voice. To my relief, the gray-haired sagamon who had greeted all the others extended that same welcome to me in a voice that sounded relieved.

“Hello, my friend,” he said, extending an open hand toward me. “Welcome. Enter as a friend and join our circle around the fire.”

CHAPTER 18

His Name Was Nadialid

"MY NAME," I SAID, "IS Wabi. My great-grandfather was from this place. His name was Nadialid."

People nodded at that.

"Nadialid?" said an old man. "There was a fine young man of that name when I was a small boy. Tall and strong he was, much as you are. But that Nadialid just went off hunting one day and never returned."

Perfect!

"Yes," I quickly said, "that is the same Nadialid who was my great-grandfather."

"Why did he never return to our village?" someone else asked.

I recognized that sweet but skeptical voice. Dojihla.

"Ah, he was taken by an urge to . . . uh, to wander," I said, both telling the truth and making things up as I went along. "To see things he had never seen before." (Such as how the world looks when you view it from the sky.) "After he met my great-grandmother, they chose each other as mates for life. His love for her was so great that he decided to stay with her and follow the ways of her people."

I smiled and looked around me. It seemed to be working. People were nodding their heads in approval. Even Dojihla seemed interested in this tale of how my great-grandfather had given up everything—more than she could imagine, in fact—to be with my great-grandmother.

"After his passing, my great-grandmother and their fledglings—uh, children—remained with . . . her own people. But his story was passed on down to me. It fascinated me. So I made the long journey to reach this place."

"Your only reason for coming to our village was to see the home of your ancestors?" asked Dojihla's father.

"Of course," I said. "What better reason could there be to come to this beautiful place?"

Several people smiled at this and one or two of the young men in the circle looked relieved. Dojihla, though, looked either disappointed or disbelieving.

"You do not know of the contest?" She spat out that last word as if it was a piece of rotten meat.

"There is a contest?" I asked in an innocent voice.

Dojihla opened her mouth to say something further, but her mother leaned in front of her.

"Young man," she said to me, "do you have a wife? Is there some young woman to whom you are promised in your home village?"

"A wife? No." I paused. How much should I say? I settled on words that I hoped would both tell the truth and hide it. "I lived alone with my great-grandmother after losing my parents."

Dojihla's mother was smiling very broadly now.

"Ah," Dojihla's father said, showing his large teeth in a grin so big that his face seemed ready to split in half. "Ah, ah, ah! But would you like to find a wife?"

I managed to control myself. I did not shout "YES!" or bob my head up and down madly. I just lifted one hand up to my chin (as I had seen Dojihla's father do while he was listening to me talk about where I came from) to indicate I was carefully considering his words.

"Yes," I said slowly, looking at the fire as I did so. "But I am not sure how to go about finding a wife. Among my own people, it is always the female who decides who her mate will be."

I didn't turn my head in Dojihla's direction as I spoke those words, but I did take advantage of the fact that my new eyes could move so freely. As I looked out of the corner of one eye, I thought that I saw her expression change for just a moment. I quickly shifted my eyes back down toward the fire.

"Young man," Dojihla's father said, placing one hand on my shoulder, "how good a hunter are you?"

I sat up and looked around. For the first time in my life, I was inside a wigwam, one of the little upside-down nests in which humans live. It was surprisingly comfortable. True, fresh breeze did not blow over me as it would have done in a proper perch high in a tree, but my human body needed more warmth from such things as clothing and fires than I had ever found necessary as an owl.

Around me I heard the sounds of sleep. All of the young men who were to hunt tomorrow had been given this one wigwam to sleep in. The sounds—and occasional smells—that they gave off were... interesting. All of them were sleeping soundly, but I was too excited, too unused to sleeping during the best part of the night, to keep my eyes closed. Plus, I now realized that there were some other questions I needed to have answered.

It was easy to move silently from the lodge and slip out of the village without anyone noticing me. I was pleased to realize that, although my eyes were weaker at night than they had once been, I could still see well enough to move quickly through the trees. Soon I was not walking, but running. My new legs were well made for such exercise. I felt as if I could run all night.

Suddenly, a dark, growling shape leaped at me from the forest, knocking me off balance. A long-toothed mouth gaped wide at me. Hot breath blew in my face. There was only one thing I could do.

"Get off," I said.

Malsumsis woofed and then hopped off to one side.

"Idiot!" I scratched my wolf friend's ears with the fingers of my hands and he whined happily. "Yes," I said, "I am glad to see you too."

The two of us began to run together through the forest. I had never been able to run with my friend before, only swooped on silent wings over his head. I liked the feeling of our running together, the soft thump of the earth beneath us, the way the ground seemed to rise up to catch me each time I lifted a foot and let it fall. The night wind in our faces was sweet. I'd been eager to reach the tree where I knew my great-grandmother would be roosting, but it was almost too soon when we arrived there. This running was so much fun.

As soon as I called her name, she came swooping down.

"Whoooo-whoooo," she said. "Wabi, there is more that you need."

It was not a question. As always, it was as if she knew my thoughts.

"Yes, Great-grandmother," I said. "I forgot that humans are not like owls when they hunt."

I looked down at my feet—so good for running, so pathetically useless for such things as striking and killing prey. "I need something to hunt with."

Great-grandmother chuckled. "I know," she said. "I would have told you before, but you were toooo eager to go." She nodded her beak toward an old, old maple tree. "Look inside the hollow of that tree."

I went to the maple. Its hollow was a narrow slit, but I was able to reach my arm far inside. Even without seeing, my sensitive human fingers were able to find what was hidden there. I pulled it out. It was a long object wrapped in old worn deerskin, just as my clothing had been. I undid the laces that tied it to disclose a fine bow with its double-twisted string wrapped about it, a quiver of arrows. I placed them carefully on the deerskin and stood back to look at them. I knew that they had been in that tree for many, many seasons, yet they glistened like new in the light from the full face of the moon. Nadialid's own weapons.

CHAPTER 19

Stringing the Bow

WHEN THE SUN LIFTED AGAIN into the sky, it found me asleep, really asleep, inside the wigwam in Valley Village along with the dozen other young men. In fact, I was the last of them to wake. The clouds at the edge of the sky had already begun to show the first streaks of red when I had finally slipped back in among the snoring suitors. I had spent much of the night learning to use my new weapons.

But the voices of the young men woke me.

"What is wrong with Gwanakwozid over there?" I heard one of them say.

Gwanakwozid? The Long Tall One? Who is that?

"Hah, he is probably one of those who just looks like a good hunter but is really a lazy fool," another voice said. "Let him remain there like a dead log."

"Too late. Look, he's moving."

"Slowly, though. You would think from the way he acts that it's time to sleep and not the dawn."

Ah, they were talking about me. Little did they know how true those last words actually were.

I sat up, rubbing my eyes against the light. The other suitors were chuckling as they went out the door of the wigwam. I stood, rearranged my feathers—er, clothes—and followed them outside.

The others in the village were eating. It was food that had been damaged by hot water and burned by their fires. Some of it was not even meat. Yet it smelled good to my human nose. My impulse was to hop over to the pots and help myself, but I was cautious.

Watch what the others do. Learn from them.

I noticed that the other young men from the guest lodge looked as hungry as I felt. But none of them went over to take food. Dojihla's father, who was also the village leader, came to stand before us. Wowadam, He Who Knows. That was his name.

"The job of the hunter," Wowadam said, "is to feed the people. So none of you will eat this day until you have finished your hunt. Are you all ready to begin?"

He looked at each of the young men who stood there, their bows and arrows held out before them for his inspection. He stopped in front of me.

"Wabi, great-grandson of Nadialid," he said, "where are your weapons?"

"To show that I came here as a friend," I said, "I did not bring them with me. I left them hidden just outside the village."

“Ah-hah,” Dojihla’s father said. He looked relieved. “Run and get them,” he said.

Run, he said. I ran swiftly from the village to the cedar tree just within the forest. I reached up into its branches to grasp the bundle that held the unstrung bow, the quiver, and the arrows. Then I returned to the place where the others still stood.

For some reason, the young men were all gaping at me. Some of the others gathered around were making gasping sounds. Others were saying such things as “Wah-hey,” and “Nanabi! So fast!”

Dojihla, though, was just looking at me in a way that made me feel uneasy. Had I just run a little too swiftly?

“Wabi,” Wowadam said, “are the others of your family as fast a runner as you?”

“No,” I said, answering quite truthfully. There was no way any owl could hop as fast as I had just run.

“Ah,” he said. Then he shook his head and turned his attention to the bundle I held. “May I see your weapon?”

I unwrapped the bow and held it out in front of me. As I did so I realized for the first time that it was larger and thicker than any of the bows held by the other young men.

“That is no bow,” said the young man next to me. “That is a tree.”

“A war club, more like,” said the next young man. “Perhaps he hunts by hitting animals over the head with it.”

All of the other suitors laughed, as did many of the people gathered around.

I was beginning to get used to this kind of teasing. I had listened often enough from the forest to such talk between humans, especially young human males, to know that it was meant both playfully and, sometimes, as a challenge.

It came to me then how I could respond. I turned toward the other young men and held out my unstrung bow.

"Here," I said. "Would anyone like to try to string this?"

A large young man, a head shorter than me but a bit broader and with a face as round as that of the moon, was pushed forward by his friends.

"Go ahead, Wikadegwa," one of them said.

"Bend it until it breaks, Fat Face," said another.

Fat Face held out his hands and then smiled at me. It was a smile that showed no teeth. Somehow I knew that this smile was meant to say, *I am only doing this because they are making me do it.*

I smiled back and handed him the bow. He hefted it in his hands, then looped the string around one end, placed the other end of the bow against the ground, and leaned his back into it. The bow did not bend. Fat Face strained harder. Water began to pop out of his forehead in little bubbles. Was Fat Face's head getting ready to explode?

"WHHHAAAAGGGH!" Fat Face blew the air out of his mouth and let go of the bow. He staggered back a step before regaining his balance.

"It cannot be done," he said, handing me the bow. "No one can bend this. You are playing a joke on us all."

Everyone was looking at me. I shook my head. "It is not a joke," I said. "My great-grandfather could bend this bow." I paused and looked around. I wrapped one leg around the bow, grasped the upper end with my hand, pressed down on it, and slipped the string in place. Then I held it up and plucked it with my finger, a deep throbbing note twanging out.

"And," I said, plucking the string again, "so can I."

A chorus of "Oh-hos" and "Ahs" came from those gathered around me. Fat Face was patting my shoulder in a friendly way. The sharp-faced young man who had made the remark about my sleeping like a dead log stepped forward. I remembered his name. It was Bitahlo.

"So, you can string that thing. But can you shoot it?" he asked.

"What shall I shoot at?" I said.

"Can you hit the middle knot on that pine tree over there by the—WAGH!" He stared at my arrow quivering in the middle of the target he had just named.

"Like that?" I said.

"Ah, yes," Bitahlo said in a slow voice as he moved back into the group of young men who again appeared to be trying to catch flies with their mouths.

"I am impressed," another voice spoke up from the back of the crowd. Why did it sound familiar to me? A tall, broad-shouldered man stepped forward. He was holding a small child in his arms. Suddenly I recognized him. It was Melikigo, Dojihla's big brother. Apparently, even though he now lived in another village with his wife's family, he had come to see this contest to win his sister. As he walked toward me, Dojihla's father shook his head.

"My son," Wowadam said, "there is not time enough for this."

Melikigo grinned as he placed his child in Wowadam's arms. "Father, there is always time for a little friendly wrestling."

Wrestling. I should have expected it from him. His name Melikigo, means "He is strong." I had seen, over the years, how none of the other boys—or the men when he was grown—had ever been able to throw him.

He reached out to grasp my wrist. "Shall we try to throw each other?"

I grasped his wrist in turn. I tried to remember the words I'd heard spoken when men wrestled.

"Let us do so," I said. "Tell me when to begin."

"Now!" Melikigo shouted. His big muscles strained as he tried to pull me forward into him so that he could wrap his arms around me. I didn't move. He tried another tactic, pushing into me. This time I turned in a half circle, even though there was no way he could have moved me. He was strong, but I could feel how much stronger I was.

I did not throw him, though, even though it would not have been hard to do. Instead, I stayed locked up with him as the two of us moved back and forth. Water was now dripping from his forehead. One or two times, I pushed a little too hard and had to pull him back so that he would not lose his footing. To anyone watching, it must have looked like an even match. Melikigo, though, knew.

"Enough," he finally said. He let go of me and I released my own grip. His eyes found mine as he nodded. I understood the message in his gaze. *Thank you,* his look was saying, *for not making me appear foolish in front of my family.*

He turned to look at his sister. She had been watching us closely. I looked too, but Dojihla quickly turned her glance away from me.

"My sister," Melikigo said, reaching out his hand to thump me on the chest, "this is a good one."

"Hummph," was all that Dojihla said in reply.

CHAPTER 20
The Feast

I'D SELDOM HUNTED IN THE daylight before. Things looked different than at night. You could see your prey from much farther away—and it could see you. That all took some getting used to. I'd also never used any other weapon to hunt with than my own talons. That took even more getting used to.

But hunting with my great-grandfather Nadialid's bow and arrows had not turned out to be that difficult. For me, the hardest part about hunting that day was not finding game and shooting it. It was remembering what humans like to hunt. I had just crept close enough to the most delicious-looking chipmunk when it came to me that humans liked larger food. Forget about mice, shrews (which have a nice sharp tang to them), baby crows (yummy and crunchy). Think about animals even bigger than bunnies. Probably not skunks.

Wabi, I said to myself, think big. *Think deer. Elk. Moose. Got it?*

At first, when I found the animals I had decided to hunt, they fled from me. I had never approached anything from the ground before, but always from the air. When you hunt from the air, you move with the wind and it carries you. On the ground, a hunter's scent is carried by the wind. I finally realized that I had to approach with the wind in my face. Then they would not catch my human scent and flee.

I did not forget to show respect. Each time I took aim, I spoke the words much like those we owls always speak before we strike. *You who will feed me and my family, I thank you for giving me your life.*

My arrows hit just where I wanted them to hit. That was very satisfying. It felt almost as it used to feel when I struck not with arrows but with the claws of my owl feet.

My next challenge was moving the game I caught. Big animals cannot just be picked up in your claws and flown away with. Luckily this new body of mine was strong. Dragging worked well, although it took more time than I had planned.

As a result, it was not until the evening, as the last light was disappearing in the sunrise direction, that I walked into Dojihla's village. I was the last of the hunters to return. They were all lined up before the big fire, each with the game they had killed piled in front of them. Their take ranged from the two deer and the beaver proudly displayed by Fat Face (a better hunter than I had expected) to the single woodchuck at the feet of an embarrassed-looking Bitahlo.

Dojihla was eyeing them all with equal displeasure. But

when I stepped into the firelight and she looked at me, it seemed as if I saw a different expression come over her face.

I dropped the two big bucks I'd been carrying, one over each shoulder. Both were larger than the two Fat Face had brought.

"Two deer," Dojihla's father said.

"Plump ones," said her mother with a big smile.

Dojihla said nothing.

Oops, I thought. *Not a good sign.* But I refused to let worry get in my way—or Fat Face, who had smiled at me when I walked into the circle of light. A strange thing to do, smiling at a rival like that. He was now being poked in the back by the older woman behind him. I knew her to be his mother from the conversations they had the evening before.

"Speak up, son," she commanded.

"I, uh, I have two deer *and* a beaver," Fat Face said. "That should make me the, uh, winner?" To my further surprise, his voice was unenthusiastic.

I raised my hand. "Wait," I said. Then I walked back into the woods.

When I returned, it was with another game animal over my shoulders. I placed it next to the two deer. As I walked back into the forest I thought about the look I had seen on people's faces. Perhaps carrying a full-grown elk was a little too impressive. So this time when I returned, I did so dragging in the big bull moose by its antlers. When I straightened up I saw that everyone was staring openmouthed.

Wowadam was the first to recover. "Wabi has won," he said, placing a hand on my shoulder.

"He will be my son-in-law," Dojihla's mother said. She

wrapped her arms around me in a warm embrace. That made me feel good. However, the fact that she whispered "Be brave" in my ear did cause me a bit of disquiet.

Once again, Dojihla had nothing to say. Her eyes were not looking at me, but through me. A little shiver of uncertainty went down my spine.

But things went well at first. The other young men came over to congratulate me. They did not look disappointed.

"You are indeed a good hunter," Fat Face said.

"Where did you find an elk of that size?" Bitahlo asked.

"We must go out hunting together sometime," said a short, stocky young man who introduced himself as Gitowdeb.

As they talked with me, some of them began to confide in me. They had all been pushed into the competition by their parents, who were eager for the prestige to be gained by their son marrying the chief's daughter. I wondered if Bitahlo with his single woodchuck might have been a better hunter than I thought. Fat Face, in particular, seemed relieved that he had not won Dojihla.

"Good luck marrying a bobcat," he whispered to me.

"I do not understand," I said. And I didn't. What did a bobcat have to do with anything? It was confusing enough to have been an owl who fell in love with a human without bringing in the prospect of marrying yet another sort of animal.

"She is better suited to you," Fat Face said, chuckling as he did so. He patted me on the shoulder. "May you survive it."

Preparations moved along for the feast as I was moved from one group of happy people to the next. They were pleased by all the game I had brought in. I was pleased, too, but getting a bit dizzy.

"We will all eat well tonight," said a woman holding a baby.

"Welcome to our family, brother-to-be," said the man behind her. It was Melikigo, Dojihla's brother. He thudded me again in the chest with the flat of his palm and then slapped his hand over his heart.

"You are just the sort of hunter we need for our village," an old man said to me. He placed a string of clay beads in my hand and then looped them around my neck when I did not seem to know what to do with them.

Children were tugging at my hands or wrapping their arms around my legs, men and women of all ages were coming up to embrace me.

I began to feel as if I was caught in a strong wind that was blowing me first one way and then the other. And through it all, every time I caught Dojihla's eyes, I felt troubled by the look that I saw there. Questioning.

They sat me down in front of the fire with Dojihla by my side. Meat from the various animals I brought in had been thrust onto wooden spits and was being cooked over the fire right in front of us. Fat was dripping out and spattering on the hot coals. The smell of the cooking meat filled my nose. My mouth began to fill again with water. I swallowed. It made my nose twitch. What a strange sensation that was! It twitched again. I reached up to touch it with my fingers. This soft nose was not at all like my hard beak. I pushed it with my finger, feeling it move. So different. Yet I was getting used to it. In fact, I rather liked having this kind of a nose.

I looked over at Dojihla. I liked her nose even more than mine. Her nose was the most pleasing to look at of all the young women there. I smiled at her and she smiled back sweetly.

Too sweetly?

Suddenly, a feeling of panic swept over me. I did not know how, but I knew I was in trouble. I'd seen that look on Dojihla's face before many times, from when she was a little girl playing with her friends. Whenever she got that look, someone else—who had been doing something to displease her—was soon going to be unhappy.

What had I done? I did not know what to say or how to act. I looked around for Fat Face, hoping that he might help me. But he was in another group of people far away from us, talking with a young woman who giggled at his every word.

"Husband-to-be?" a sweet voice whispered close to my ear. Warm breath caressed my cheek. It made my heart beat faster.

I turned to look into Dojihla's eyes. My heart thudded to a stop. What I saw was far from sweetness. There was a challenge and a question, there was suspicion and stubbornness. I truly was in trouble. And I had no idea how to get out of it.

"Yes," I answered. *If you cannot think of what to say,* I thought, *say as little as possible.*

Dojihla reached up a hand to touch my face. "You are feeling too hot?" she asked.

Her innocent tone made a chill go down my back. How could I not be feeling hot with all of the logs she had been piling onto the fire next to us?

"You are very warm," she continued. One of her fingers brushed something wet from my forehead.

Warm *and* wet? I put one hand up to feel it. It was true. Moisture was leaking out of my skin. Was something wrong with me? I held my wet hand out by the fire. It wasn't blood. Then I remembered that I had seen water like this dripping from Fat Face's forehead when he tried to string my bow and from the forehead of Dojihla's brother when we wrestled.

"You are sweating so much," Dojihla said. "I am sure your headband is too hot."

"Yes," I agreed. I was feeling faint.

This time, as you have probably already guessed, saying the least was not the best. But I was confused. After all, I had not been a human for that long. When owls are hot, they don't sweat. They just pant or fan their wings.

"Then let us take that headband off," Dojihla said, reaching up both her hands.

"Yes," I said, then, "NO!"

But it was too late. Quicker than a bat snatching a moth out of the air, Dojihla whipped that leather band from around my head and my two tall owl ears popped up.

All around us, people gasped.

"Kina!" someone said. Look!

"Ears like an owl?" said another voice.

Dojihla stood and stepped back from me. Triumph gleamed in her bright eyes.

"Look," she shouted, pointing at me as she did so. "I promised I would marry the man who was the best hunter. But this one is not a man. See those ears? This one is not a human being. Perhaps he was planning to devour me as soon as he got me alone."

"Wabi," said Wowadam, "is this true?"

Dojihla grabbed her father's arm and pulled him away from me. "Do not get too close," she said. "He may try to harm you now that we have found him out to be a monster."

"Be careful," someone else shouted. It was Bitahlo. "Get away from him."

Fat Face stared at me, shaking his head.

Dojihla's mother was covering her mouth with both of her hands.

Melikigo had stepped protectively between me and his wife and baby.

My heart was breaking. I stood and looked around the circle of firelight at the shocked faces staring at me. I did not see a single look of friendship or understanding. I was a monster to them all.

I shook my head. "No-ooo-ooo," I said. "No-oo-ooo."

But that was all I could think to say. I knew as soon as I said it how I sounded. Not like a man at all. I turned, grabbed up my bow and quiver of arrows, and walked swiftly into the darkness.

CHAPTER 21

What I Needed to Do

I WAS IN GREAT PAIN. An ache had blossomed in the center of my being as soon as Dojihla had exposed me as something other than I had pretended to be. How could I have thought they would accept me as a human? *What a fool I am,* I thought as I stumbled away from Valley Village.

Stumbled, indeed. Admittedly, another part of my pain was from the big bump on my forehead. I'd gotten that by walking head-on into a large maple tree soon after I stalked out into the darkness. Not only had it spoiled the dignity of my exit (the Kabonk-Ouch! had to have been audible to all those I left behind), but it also reminded me that I no longer had the acute night vision of an owl.

I intended to go straight back to Great-grandmother's tree, but it was much harder than I expected. I didn't know where

I was. Moon was not showing her face. There was not enough light for me to find my way. What would have once been an easy flight above the trees was now so difficult. My arms and legs became caught in the brush, tangles of berry bushes grabbed at my hair and scratched my face. In my usual stubborn way, I kept pressing onward. But nothing was familiar to me in the darkness beneath the canopy of branches that had been my home territory. On and on I went, my hands held out before me to help me feel my way. It was so different from flying.

I do not know how long I walked. But I do know that gradually yet another feeling came over me. It was something I had never felt before at night. Rather than being wakeful and alert, I was becoming tired. Very tired, indeed. Even though it was the middle of the night, I had to sleep. My human legs refused to carry me any farther. I allowed them to collapse beneath me.

A familiar growl came from the darkness nearby. It was Malsumsis. His large shadow came close, and his wet nose touched my cheek. I had thought I heard something following close to me as I walked through the dark, but I had paid it no heed. I had not been afraid. Quite frankly, there was an edge of anger to my despair. I had half hoped it was some unfriendly being planning to attack me. I was looking forward to such a fight. Any creature thinking I was no more than a weak and foolish human would be surprised.

Instead, it had been my only loyal friend. He had kept pace with me, waiting for the moment when he could give me comfort. He'd been waiting for me in the forest all the time I was in the village. Even though I was not the same Wabi he'd known before, Malsumsis still cared for me.

My vision began to blur. It was almost as if my second eyelids had returned. But that was not it. My eyes grew warmer, moister. I put my hands up and felt the water trickling out of them, down my cheeks onto my chin. Why was I sweating from my eyes? I had not realized that human beings had so much water in them that it came leaking out from so many places. Somehow, though, that moisture coming from my eyes seemed suited to the way I felt. I had never, ever been so sad before.

I pressed my face against Malsumsis's side, wrapped my arms around him. Then I slept.

When I opened my eyes again, Malsumsis was gone, but the gentle touch of darkness was still around me. And I heard a soft voice.

"Whoo-hoo-hoo," it trilled. "Grandson."

I squinted my eyes and looked around. The moon had finally risen and her bright light shone through the trees. I could see enough to make out the shape of my great-grandmother on a branch near me. Although I thought I had been lost in the darkness, I had found my way to her tree, which I now realized was rising above me. I had fallen asleep in the circle of stones, right next to that same bed of moss where I'd first stretched out my new fingers.

"Grandmother," I said. Then I was silent. I did not know what else to say and I could not think of even one question to ask. All I could think of was how sad I felt, how lonely.

Great-grandmother hopped down to me and leaned over to gently nibble my earlobe. Then she began to run her beak through my tangled hair. I closed my eyes, remembering what it was like when I was a little owlet and she had preened my feathers in just this way. It didn't take away the pain that had settled like a sharp bone in my stomach, but it did make me feel calmer. I lifted up my hand to wipe my face. For some reason, even though the night was cool, that warm sweat was again leaking from my eyes.

"Those are tears, Wabi. You are crying."

I looked at my great-grandmother. I had no idea how old she was, how many winters she had lived through or how many more she would survive. I was certain there could be no one who knew more, no being who had gained more wisdom. I needed wisdom just then.

"What must I do now?" I asked.

Great-grandmother clicked her beak in pleasure. "Good, grandson. Now I know it is you. You are asking questions again."

"But who am I? Am I a human being or an owl or am I an owl pretending to be a human or am I only half a human being who can never be an owl again or . . ."

Great-grandmother nodded her head. "You are Wabi," she said. "And as far as what you must do, that is up to yoooou."

I stood up and began walking in a circle. Somehow, that felt as normal for me to do as shifting from one foot to the other had felt when I was an owl. I shook my head as I circled. It seemed that whether I was a human or an owl, I still could not stop myself from thinking so much that I became confused. I needed to stop talking and thinking. I needed to do something.

Malsumsis came trotting back into the circle of stones, a fat rabbit held in his jaws. He plopped down on his haunches in front of me, dropped the dead rabbit at my feet, and looked up at me.

Food. You need to eat.

Here I had been feeling sorry for myself while he was thinking about my well-being. Malsumsis was a better friend than I deserved.

Then it came to me what I should do. It was something that had been at the back of my mind for a long time. As an owl, I had been reticent to fly far beyond my own hunting territory. Now, I realized, I felt different. As a human, the thought of doing something that might mean much travel seemed not only easier, but desirable and even necessary to me. More important, it would take me out of this valley. Right now, the thought of remaining so close to the one I loved who rejected me was too painful. I needed to be far away from those I had once thought of as my human beings, those who now feared me as if I was some kind of monster.

"Great-grandmother," I said. "I know what I must do now. I must go and try to find out what happened to my wolf friend's people."

"Wabi," she replied, "that is gooood."

CHAPTER 22

The Wide Valley

I LOOKED BACK FROM THE narrow pass between the mountains and held up my hand as I had seen real humans do to measure the passing of the sun across the sky. It had moved three times the width of my hand since we had started our climb from the valley below. I was now higher above the valley than I had ever been before. Even when I had the wings of an owl, I had never flown this high. Here I could look out across the whole of the place that had always been my home.

Malsumsis leaned his head against my thigh. I reached down absentmindedly to the place between his ears where he always wanted me to scratch. I could not see Valley Village itself, but the smoke that rose up from their fires was clearly visible above the trees. There, above the village, was the waterfall, and, here and there, like the body of a snake half hidden in brush, was the river. It was at the river that I had first seen Dojihla. Tears came into my eyes and I wiped them away.

I turned my gaze a bit farther up the valley. I was able to pick out the top of the old tree where I knew my great-grandmother was roosting.

I would not be returning there soon. Perhaps not at all. I turned my back on the familiar valley that held, with the exception of my wolf companion, everything that I had ever cared for. My journey was taking me another way, to a place so unfamiliar that I had no idea what to expect—other than one thing: danger.

It was from this distant valley that most of the creatures that threatened the humans came. Toad Woman, when she fled our valley, had headed for the very pass where I now stood. Kaskigenhana. Wide Valley. That was what the humans I left behind called it. But no humans ever went there—or if they did, they did not come back.

It was also through this pass that the whole wolf pack of our own valley had disappeared when Malsumsis was only a puppy. I'd learned that from forest creatures who'd preferred answering questions to being eaten. Foxes and fishers, woodchucks and skunks were among those who'd taken note of the wolves. They had seen or scented them as they passed by, the whole pack moving as silently as a dream.

Without looking back, those wolves had climbed the slope, higher than any sensible being would go, then vanished through this gap between the high peaks. It was strange.

Animals avoided climbing up to this pass. Even the hawks and eagles that flew high above our valley never turned their wings in the direction of Kaskigenhana.

I had learned all of that many seasons ago and had promised myself that I would find out more about it someday. I would discover what happened to Malsumsis's relatives. But as an owl, I had always been too busy with other things, including observing the humans in general and one human female in particular. But now, now all of that was behind me.

I studied this land that was as new to my human eyes as being human was to me. Some of Kaskigenhana appeared familiar—the comforting green of thick forest much like the valley woods I was leaving behind. What was strange was that even though this valley was at least four times as large as my home valley, the total amount of woodland here was much smaller.

There were several meadows where beavers had made dams in the streams. I had always liked beaver meadows. Lots of voles and mice there to hunt. But as I squinted my eyes to see more clearly, I noticed that those dams did not seem to be in good condition. And the beaver lodges that rose above the surface of the ponds appeared to be broken.

There was also a smaller range of hills within the valley, much like those in our home. The rocks on those hills would make good lookout points for me.

But at the far end of Wide Valley things were different—unsettlingly so. There was a greater expanse of swampland than I had ever seen before. Beyond that swamp there was no more forest. Instead, the land there seemed torn and was blackened as if by fire.

Malsumsis growled. *Not good.*

I nodded my head in agreement. I felt it too.

As Malsumsis and I looked out across Kaskigenhana, something was looking back at us from that burned, far end of the valley. And not in a friendly way.

CHAPTER 23
Head Breaker

I TOOK A FEW STEPS down the slope toward the valley. Then I stopped. I needed to think about a few things. I still felt the sorrow in my heart that had pierced me like an arrow when I was rejected by Dojihla. However, the pain did not seem so great now. It was still with me, but it no longer clouded my vision nor slowed my steps. It was still pain, but it was no longer sharp.

That was good. That sharp pain had made me confused and uncertain. It is never good to be confused and uncertain when you are flying—walking, I mean, toward danger.

I sat down and Malsumsis sat beside me. I put my arm around him and he thumped his tail against the ground, making a sound like that of one of the drums the people of Valley Village had been playing at the feast to honor my victory. I had liked the sound of those drums and the singing they had been doing. It was not as good as owl singing, but it had not been bad. If you are ever going to be transformed into another creature, make sure it is a creature that sings. Life without song is not good at all.

I began to tap my hand against the ground, trying to remember the beat of those drums and the song they had been singing before Dojihla pulled off my headband. It was a song of friendship. The words came to me and I began to sing them softly.

"Wi gai wah neh, wi gai wah neh."

The more I sang it, the more I liked that song. And it made me remember the warm feeling I had always held for those human beings. As foolish as they were at times, they were likeable creatures. I just wished, now that I had become one of them, that they liked and trusted me.

But there was nothing I could do about that now. Perhaps an idea would come to me later. The important thing was that I not just sit around and feel sorry for myself. I had set a task for myself. That was good. That task was going to be difficult and dangerous. That made it even better.

But I did not have to rush into it. I looked down into the wide valley again. What was waiting for me there? Was I prepared for it? I had dealt with treacherous creatures before when I was an owl, but how was I equipped now to deal with them as a human being? I needed to think about that.

I looked at myself. No wings. That meant I could not fly out of danger if I needed to do so. Nor could I drop heavy stones from high above. But I did have my bow and my arrows. My new hands felt comfortable with that bow and those arrows that had belonged to my great-grandfather. When I held them, it was as if I was holding his hands. It was also as if they were a part of me. I could use those arrows to strike any enemy from a safe distance.

My hands were good for other things too. I could hold things and throw them. I picked up a large rock, pulled my arm back, and hurled the stone as hard as I could. It sailed far away and dropped out of sight into the valley below. I would have to practice to throw accurately, but I could see that this skill would be of great help.

What other weapons did I have? I looked down. I no longer had talons on my feet that could rip and tear. My feet were good for running, but what else? Perhaps for kicking? Moose and deer use their feet very effectively that way. I had once seen a medium-sized doe use her feet to drive away a full-grown mountain lion when it tried to grab her fawn.

Kicking.

There was a dead cedar tree that stood about three times my height just down the slope from me. I sat back and picked up one of my feet to lift it up to my opposite knee. I was getting used to having knees that bent forward. I pulled off my moccasin and studied that foot. I now had not four toes, but five. They were not of equal size or able to move around to grasp anything. I used my fingers to bend those stiff, small toes backward and forward. If I bent too far, it hurt. They were not strong like my former toes had been. The nails on them were no use at all for fighting. If I struck these new toes against something hard, they would have no effect. They could not even pierce a mouse's skin. But the bottom of my foot was different. It seemed to be tough and solid. It might work.

I put my moccasin back on and walked over to the tree. I gave it a push with my hand. It was rooted solidly into the stone and thin earth of the mountainside. It would be a good test for me. I stepped back, took a deep breath, lifted my knee up high, and then thrust my foot out to hit the trunk of that cedar as hard as I could.

THWACK!

Splinters flew as the tree broke off near its base, toppled, and rolled down the slope.

"Whoo-hoo-hooo," I shouted in triumph. My foot tingled a bit, but was not hurt at all.

Kicking, I thought. *Good weapon for me!*

Malsumsis came leaping back up the hill. He had run down after the big dead cedar as it rolled, and he was now carrying one of its broken branches in his mouth. He dropped it at my feet.

I picked it up and threw it, and Malsumsis went springing after it, caught it on the first bounce, and came back to my feet again. This time, though, instead of dropping the branch, he nudged me with it. I took it more carefully from his teeth, held it up, and hefted it. It felt good in my hand. It was smooth and the length of my arm. It had broken off cleanly and one end was heavier and more rounded. I had seen the men of Valley Village carrying such branches. What was it they called them?

Baskodebahiganak. Head Breakers. That was it. Fighting clubs.

I grasped my fighting club by the narrow end and swung it

back and forth a few times. It made a whistling sound as it cut through the air. Very good, indeed. Head Breaker. Another weapon. But as I swung it I realized I was forgetting something.

I walked over to what was left of the broken old cedar, put down my new club, and placed my hands on the base of the trunk.

"You have given me a gift," I said to the tree. "I thank you for Head Breaker. I will carry it with me and use it well."

CHAPTER 24

Big Crows

THE MOUNTAIN SLOPE BELOW US was strewn with stones of all sizes. I studied that slope, trying to pick out the best path for us to get through the jumble of rocks to the valley below.

I shook my head. It would not be easy. More than one trail led down from the mountaintop and it seemed as if some of those trails were dead ends. While in some spots there were narrow spaces between them that I thought we could squeeze through, in others big boulders had rolled together, blocking the way. Not only that, in the open places the small broken stones looked as if they would slip and slide underfoot. That would make it hard for us to move down quickly across them.

I lifted my hand to shade my eyes. You must stay alert if you wish to stay alive. Had I seen something in the air at the far end of the valley? I had. Something was moving across the low sky. It was like a cloud that kept changing shape and getting larger.

Hah-hoo. It was not a cloud at all. It was a flock of birds, coming straight this way. That was not good. They were flying swiftly. They would reach this spot where we stood, fully exposed, long before we could make our way down to the forest at the foot of the slope. That was worse. But worst of all was that I could now make out what kind of birds were in that flock. Crows. Big crows.

Malsumsis growled. The hair rose up on the back of his neck and he took half a step backward.

"Yes," I said. "I agree. They are not coming to greet us as friends."

Crows. Any owl will tell you that being caught by a mob of crows during the daytime is a terrible thing. They made me so uneasy that my first thought was to spread my wings and soar back down into my home valley where I knew the safe roosting places. I lifted my arms to open my wings. Oops.

Arms, I thought. *Flying is not an option.*

I looked at my arms and hands. *Useless for flying.* Then I smiled. *But very useful for certain other things.*

First, though, I would need a place that was not out in the open like this.

I spotted a possibility, and went quickly down the slope with Malsumsis by my side. The cloud of crows was getting closer. I could now hear what they were calling back and forth to one another in self-satisfied tones.

Gawh gah! Gawh gah!

Soon! Soon! Pluck their eyes out!

Gawh gah! Gawh gah!

Soon! Soon! Pluck their eyes out!

The place I'd seen turned out to be even better than I had hoped. Three big flat rocks had slid together in such a way that they made a shape like one of the rough, bark shelters I had seen human beings make. Agwanbitigan, they called it. A lean-to. But this one was made of stone. There was plenty of room inside for me to stand up and for Malsumsis to crouch down by my side.

One of the worst things about being mobbed by crows is the way they circle and dive around you like an evil, black-feathered whirlwind. No way could they circle us here. There was stone over our heads and stone at our backs. They could still see us as they approached. The open side of our lean-to faced out over the valley. But I was glad of that. I was ready and waiting for them.

The flock was so close now that the harsh cries hurt my ears. These were the biggest crows I'd ever seen. Their wings were as wide as those of turkey buzzards. Their glistening black beaks were long and sharp.

Gawh gah! Gawh gah!

Soon! Soon! Pluck their eyes out!

Gawh gah! Gawh gah!

Soon! Soon! Pluck their eyes out!

There were perhaps fifty of them. They were so large that I thought they must be the monster birds that served as spies for evil beings in Great-grandmother's stories. But seeing just how large they were made me feel happy.

"Bigger crows," I said to Malsumsis, whose growl was now a deep continuous rumbling in his throat, "make better targets."

Did I forget to mention another of the fine features of our shelter? Close by it were countless stones. Some were round as fists, some were flat and sharp edged, but many of them were the perfect size. I ran about, gathering a pile of them.

The crows were close enough now for me to see the hungry glint in their dark eyes. They were so close that they were starting to fold their wings to dive in at us. Close enough to throw my first stone.

Alas, my aim was not good. I completely missed the crow I'd been aiming at. However, the fact that my stone struck the crow next to it was some consolation.

Whomp! Gwark! And with a burst of feathers, that crow dropped out of the air.

My next stone hit the bird I aimed for. So did my third stone. My fourth stone, larger, rounder, and more sharp edged, was hurled in a side-arm motion. It took out not one crow but three as it spun through the rapidly diminishing flock.

They squawked at me in protest as they flew back and forth, getting ready to swirl in for another attack.

Gah-ghak! Gah-ghak!

Unfair! Unfair!

Garh-gahnk! Garh-gahnk!

Stand still and die!

Not in this lifetime, I thought, gathering up another armful of stones. It worked well that way, using one arm and hand to hold the stones cradled against my chest and doing all of my throwing with the other arm.

As I straightened up, one crow that was braver or more foolish than the others came swooping straight at my face. I did not have time to throw the stone I was holding. I turned my head to protect my eyes. But the crow did not reach me.

UURRUFF! CHOMP.

Malsumsis, my protector, dropped back down onto all fours. The body of the huge crow he had just snatched out of the air hung from his jaws. He shook it one more time and dropped it.

"Good, my friend," I said.

I would have patted him on the head, but I was too busy throwing stones again to do so. Those giant crows were determined. By the time their attack was done, the slope in front of our lean-to was covered with black-winged bodies. There were cuts on both of my arms and a slash across my cheek. Malsumsis was bleeding from more than one place on his body. But neither of us was badly hurt.

In the sky above the valley were the shapes of four surviving crows, growing smaller as they winged their way back to wherever they came from. Perhaps they could not hear me, but I still shouted out my message just the same.

"Wabi is here! Tell that to the one who sent you!"

CHAPTER 25

The Deep Spring

WHEN YOU ARE HEADED INTO danger, you do not always think about the danger that is headed away from you. That is probably why Malsumsis and I did not notice, as we made our way down into the wide valley that something else was happening at the very same time. A creature that had been watching from behind us turned and made its way downslope. But not toward us. The slope it followed led down into the valley we had left behind.

We left the crows where they lay. I thought about eating one or two of them, but decided that I was not that hungry. Crow meat is tough and unpleasant. Malsumsis clearly felt the same. When we reached the place where small plants began to grow up out of the first soil below the rocky mountainside, he bit the end of a small branch from a pine tree and walked along chewing it for a while. He wanted to get the taste of those foul birds out of his mouth.

As I picked my way down the steep slope with my bow and quiver slung over my shoulder, I held Head Breaker in my other hand. It felt unusually heavy. In the heat of our battle with those huge crows I had forgotten about my club.

Is it possible for a piece of wood to feel resentful? I wondered.

I stopped and held Head Breaker up in front of my face.

"My friend," I said, "I am sorry that you were not included in our last battle. Rest assured that you will not be neglected next time."

I looked down into the valley below us, feeling that invisible but baleful presence again.

"I think you will not have to wait for long," I added. Then I swung Head Breaker in a wide circle. It no longer felt so heavy in my hand. If anything, it felt as if it were pulling me along down the trail that now opened before us.

Before long, we were in the forest. But it was like no forest I had been in before. True, there were trees and small plants, flowers and berries, just as in the forests of our home valley. The little flying and crawling creatures were here as well. A grasshopper chirruped as it flew up from the grass, bees hummed in the blossoms.

But there were no larger creatures. No birds, no animals. I saw none, nor did I smell any. My human nose was weaker than that of my wolf companion's, but I could tell from the look on his face that he too found that lack of familiar scents confusing. It was as if the ground, or something worse, had swallowed up all the birds and animals.

It worried me in two ways. My smaller worry was about

food. I'd thought that the two of us could hunt and eat before going farther. But with no animals here, what would we hunt? My larger worry was about what had happened to the creatures that should have been here. Would whatever happened to them now happen to us?

I was thirsty too. In fact, I felt a stronger thirst than I had ever felt before. Luckily, there was a lovely pool of water before us. From the sand at its bottom and the bubbles that rose up in it, it seemed to be water from a spring. Such water always tastes better. The water was so clear that I could see there were many round white pebbles at the bottom, resting on the golden sand.

How good it will feel, I thought as I quickened my pace, to kneel by that spring. *Go closer, go closer! First, though, I must throw aside my weapons. Go closer, go closer! And then I must blindly thrust my arms and head into that cool, sweet water. Closer, closer! I must do that, I must...*

I must not! I forced my feet to stop walking while I was still a stone's throw away from the water. I quickly reached out my hand and grabbed hold of the scruff of Malsumsis's neck to stop him from walking on just as foolishly as I had been doing. My wolf friend looked back at me, confused. Then he growled and sat back on his haunches. He shook his head and wiped his face with his paws. I knew how he felt. It was as if he'd just blundered into a spiderweb that had obscured his vision for a moment.

Go closer, go closer? Why was I thinking that? And what was that about throwing my weapons aside? Ha! Thrust my head and arms into the water? Not likely!

Whose voice had been speaking in my head, trying to convince me to behave like a brainless little owlet? I took another step toward that inviting pool of water.

Come closer, come closer!

There it was again, a hungry whisper. I was fully aware of it now. It was like the subtle touch of a blood-drinking fly on your body just before it begins to drink. But this hunger, subtle as it was, was much bigger than that of a deer fly or a mosquito. It wanted more than just a sip of blood.

I stepped just a little closer. Now I could better see the pool of spring water before me. The water was much deeper than I had thought at first. I could tell that by how long it took for the bubbles to emerge from the sandy bottom and reach the surface. Those glistening white pebbles at the bottom were larger than they seemed. Then I saw what they were. They were not pebbles at all, but skulls. Skulls picked clean of all flesh. Skulls of animals and human beings.

I studied the ground around that pool. There were old tracks there, tracks of many kinds of creatures. Every set of tracks led to the pool. None led away.

I looked over at Malsumsis. The small rumble of a growl was coming from the back of his throat.

I made a small hand gesture to him. Since we had been traveling together, he and I had been learning how I could use these new human hands in more subtle ways than the wings I once had. I could make all kinds of gestures with them, signals for my wolf friend to do certain things. A hand lifted up to my mouth meant *Be quiet.* The two long fingers of my hand held together and thrust forward meant *Go that way.* All the fingers of my hand spread wide and my arm flung forward as if throwing a stone—*Attack!*

Now my palm was down, pressed toward the earth. *Wait here and be watchful.*

I unslung my bow and arrows and placed them on the ground.

"No need for these while I'm drinking water," I said in a loud voice. "And I am so thirsty." But as I walked forward, I did not drop Head Breaker in my hand. I held my club concealed behind my back.

I went down on one knee at the edge of the pool, and reached one hand toward the water. The surface trembled as my fingers touched it. Hunger rippled up from something hiding under the bank beneath me. *Bend farther. Come closer, come closer!* But I didn't move. I just kept my hand there, the way I had seen humans dangle a line in the water with a hook and a fat grub on it to entice a trout to strike.

Suddenly a long-fingered, hairy hand thrust out of the water to snatch at my wrist. But before it could grasp me firmly, I twisted my own hand around to grab it! It tried to pull me in. I had braced myself too firmly. I planted the butt of Head Breaker into the earth, straightened my back. Now it tried to free itself, to pull away, to break my grip. It could not do so. My grip had been strong when I was an owl and I was pleased to feel that same strength now.

No, you will not get away! I thought.

I yanked hard. It came snaking out from under the bank. Standing as I did so, I swung my arm back and let go, hurling the hairy creature onto the ground behind me. It landed with a heavy, soggy thud.

"GAARRRRGGGLBBLLL-URP!"

The creature's bubbly growl and its attempt to roll to its wide, webbed feet and hurl itself at me were cut short by Malsumsis. My wolf friend leaped onto the creature's chest, driving it back to the ground. Malsumsis opened his mouth and growled, his large teeth glittering only a hand's width away from the monster's throat. It was caught, pinned down by my wolf friend's paws like a rabbit held by a fox.

I do not mean that this creature was small as a rabbit. Far from it. It was at least the size of a big human being. But I may have neglected to mention just how large my wolf friend is, even for a wolf. When Malsumsis stands on his back legs and puts his front paws on my shoulders, his head towers over me.

I stepped closer to look down at what we had captured. I'd heard about such creatures. It was a gelabago, one of those monsters that lives in certain deep springs, waiting to pull in any unwary creature that comes to drink.

But no one seemed to know much about the actual look of a gelabago. No story that I'd overheard ever spoke of anyone actually seeing such a monster and surviving to talk about it. Then again, who would want to talk about something as ugly and unpleasant as this creature? It was covered with dark hair that was tight to its skin and glistened like that of a beaver. It had very long, hard muscled arms, which were very effectively pressed to the ground by Malsumsis's paws. Its hands looked soft, its skinny, pale fingers almost boneless as they continued to twitch while it lay there. But I knew that when those fingers were wrapped around something, their grip would be terribly strong. The creature's body was short, round, and flabby. It didn't need muscles there, I suppose. Its legs were short too, and its wide feet were webbed like the feet of a muskrat. In fact, it smelled a bit like a muskrat: fishy.

Its head was rounded, its forehead sloped back, it had no real nose, just two nostrils in the center of its face. Its mouth, which it kept opening and closing, was so big that when it was fully open it could probably gape wide enough to take in the head of a bear. It was just waiting for a chance to snap at Malsumsis. But Malsumsis could see that too. Any move would result in my wolf friend grabbing its throat.

"Hold," I said. "Hold."

Malsumsis lowered his head a finger's width closer to the throat of the gelabago.

It stared at me with large, cold eyes, eyes like those of a fish, but with more intelligence—but not a lot more, perhaps. There was more greedy hunger in this creature than deep thought. Lure your victim in, grab it, drown it, eat it. That was the life of a gelabago.

I picked up my bow, nocked an arrow to the string, drew it back, and pointed it at the creature's chest.

"If I shoot you," I said, "you will do no more eating."

It tried to squirm free when I said that. A growl from Malsumsis stopped it. The hunger in the gelabago's eyes slowly began to be replaced by uncertainty.

"Answer my questions and I will not shoot you," I said. "There is a powerful being in this valley. I feel its bad mind. Who is the one who holds that power?"

The gelabago opened its mouth wide. Its thick black tongue came out to lick its thin lips. But it was not from hunger. It was afraid to speak the name.

"Speak or I will let loose this arrow," I said. "Who holds power here?"

"Winasosiz," it croaked. "Oldold Woman. She holds the power. She is Winasosiz. *Come closer, come closer!*"

I stepped back. "Good. Now I have one more question. This one is for my friend. Have you eaten any wolves?"

Malsumsis's growl became a rumble like that of thunder in a growing storm.

"No," the gelabago gurgled. "Oldold Woman has them. Yes, oh yes. She has all the wolves."

I was standing between the gelabago and its pool. I looked back over my shoulder into the deep water and at those white skulls at the bottom. It seemed to be true. None of those skulls looked like those of wolves.

I did not turn back toward the loathsome creature that had drowned and devoured so many innocent victims. I had to look no further to discover why this part of the Wide Valley forest was so empty of life and why the gelabago's belly was so large.

"You have spoken the truth," I said. "I will not shoot you. Malsumsis, let the creature go."

I did not look back, but I heard the soft thump as Malsumsis leaped from on top of the monster he had pinned to the ground.

Just as I expected, the creature showed no gratitude for my keeping my word and not shooting it with an arrow. With a gurgling roar, it leaped at my back. Its plan was a simple one: Knock me into the water, pull me under. There it would be out of reach of my wolf friend's jaws. I had expected that too.

What I hadn't expected was that its leap would be so swift. For so large and ungainly a creature, it moved very fast. However, more important, I was faster in this case. Also, I'd picked my club up with my right hand as I placed my bow down with my left. Head Breaker was not about to be neglected this time.

I still kept my word. Spinning around and cracking a monster's skull with a heavy club is, after all, far different from shooting it with an arrow.

CHAPTER 26
In the Cave

AS WE CONTINUED DEEPER INTO the heart of the valley, the forest around us began to change. The first trees we had seen had mostly been those that keep their coats of green all through the cycle of the seasons. Now wider-leaved trees were around us, maples whose winged seeds provide food for many creatures, oaks and beech whose nuts are eaten by the deer and the squirrels and the mice. When I was an owl, such forests as this had been favorite places for me. Good hunting.

The change was not only in the trees. We began to see tracks and hear the sounds of small creatures rustling in the leaves and the grass. That was a relief to hear. Although the gelabago had wiped out all of the animals around its pool, there was still life other than monsters to be found in Wide Valley.

The sky, though, began to darken. Distant thunder started rolling, and soon arrows of lightning would strike.

I thought of the tales about the bedagiak, the Thunder Beings. I had heard those stories being shared by the humans of Valley Village around the fires at night while I hid in the nearby cedars. The bedagiak were beings shaped like giant humans who hunted for monsters with their fiery arrows. When their arrows struck the earth, it was to cleanse it of evil.

I had liked hearing those tales, even though I knew the real story. Great-grandmother had told it to me when I was young. The Thunder Beings were not men, but great birds. How else could they fly across the sky?

Sometimes, if innocent humans (or owls) were in the wrong place, they might be accidentally harmed or even destroyed by those fiery arrows the Thunder Beings hurled. Malsumsis and I needed to find shelter. It was becoming difficult to see in the heavy rain, which was now mixing with hard little balls of ice. The rumble of thunder was getting closer. There in front of us was a huge old tree, as big around as a human lodge. It was broken off at the top and hollow at the bottom. Malsumsis started to trot toward it. I grabbed him with both hands by the scruff of his neck and pulled him back.

"No, my friend!" I shouted to make myself heard over the splash of rain, the spatter of the hail, and the whistling of the wind. "Not a good place!"

There was nothing that I could see with my eyes, nothing that I could smell with my nose. And, of course, with the noise of the storm, nothing I could hear. But I felt a wrongness there. Inside that hollow tree was danger that we should not approach.

We staggered in the opposite direction from the big hollow tree. It was the part of the valley where we had seen the roll of hills. The side of one of those rocky hills came into view. In it was the mouth of a cave.

"There," I shouted, pulling Malsumsis toward the cave.

As soon as we tumbled inside, falling down on the dry, sandy earth beneath the wide overhang of stone, the screaming of the wind and the roar of the heavy downpour diminished.

Malsumsis shook himself so hard that water sprayed in all directions and it made me laugh. Then he sat down on his haunches facing away from the cave entrance. I wiped the rain from my face, and shook it from my soaked hair just as my wolf friend had done.

Sheets of rain washed across the mouth of the cave. It was hard to see far outside, although now and then I could make out faintly the shape of that huge broken oak. It looked even more ominous now from a distance. It was good that we had not taken shelter there. If we had entered that tree, we would not have been alone. I was certain now that something was inside that hollow tree, something not at all pleasant.

Then I realized that we were not alone here either. My sense of smell was no longer drowned by the rain, and I could smell something, something other than Malsumsis's moist fur. Malsumsis, of course, had noticed it long before I did. His nose was better than mine. That was why he was staring so intently at the back of the cave. I turned slowly to look behind us. It was not a deep cave, but it was so shadowed at the back that it was hard to make out what was crouched and hiding there.

Malsumsis was not growling as he would if there was danger. In fact, he was gently moving his tail back and forth. And that was when I too recognized the scent that had reached my nose.

I held out my hands. "We are friends," I said in a soft voice. "Come here."

A small whimper came from the back of the cave that was answered by a yelp from my wolf friend. A pale shape lifted itself up and came forward, head down, tail tucked between its legs. It dropped onto its side and then rolled onto its back at our feet, exposing its throat in the ancient sign of friendship and submission. It was not as large as my friend, and where his fur was black as night, hers was as white as snow. But there was no mistaking what it was: another wolf.

Malsumsis nudged the smaller wolf with his paw, gently grasped her by the throat with his jaws, shook once gently and then let go. *Sister, we accept your friendship.*

The female wolf jumped to her feet. Wagging her tail, she shoved her wet nose against my leg, then ran in a circle around us, whining and barking. Malsumsis kept his dignity, even though I sensed that in another place at another time he would also have been running and leaping, as happy to see her as she clearly was to find herself confronted not by enemies or monsters, but by new friends. Finally, she calmed down enough to sit back on her haunches, madly wagging her tail.

I squatted down, my back to the cave mouth that was still veiled by the wash of the rain and wind. I did not reach out to pet her as I did Malsumsis. Her submission had been to him, not to me. It would take her some time to accept me as fully as she did another wolf. But I already liked her. That crazy energy of her greeting had told me something about her personality.

"Wigowzo," I said to the female wolf as she lolled her tongue out of her mouth and smiled at Malsumsis. "You are happy indeed."

But there was more I needed to know about her than her good nature. If, as I suspected, she was one of Malsumsis's lost pack, then why was she alone? Where were the other wolves? The gelabago had spoken of a being he had called Winasosiz, the old, old woman, who had all of the wolves. What did it mean that she had all of them? And why was Wigowzo not with them?

Suddenly, there was a great flash of light and the world exploded around us.

CHAPTER 27
Cooking Meat

I ROLLED BACK UP TO my feet and looked out of the cave. The lightning strike had not hit us, but it had been so close that my head hurt and my ears were still filled with a high trilling sound like the singing of frogs. Malsumsis was crouched on his belly with his head down, snarling and ready to fight back against whatever had just attacked us. Wigowzo was pressed close to his side, both of her front paws over her eyes. Although she was as big as many grown wolves, I could see how young she was, still little more than a puppy. This might have been the first time she had ever heard such loud thunder or seen the strike of lightning so close.

I made a motion with my hand. "Be calm, my friends," I said. "That arrow of fire was not meant for us." I turned my head toward the outside. "Look there."

Malsumsis stood and came to stand by my side. After a moment's hesitation, Wigowzo did the same. The rain was letting up, the rumble of the thunder moving away from us. Across the clearing from us, the huge hollow oak tree was now blackened and burning from inside. That arrow of lightning had struck right into its heart. The air was filled with the scent of not just burning wood, but also cooking meat.

That brought a smile to my face. Whatever had been lurking inside that hollow tree was certainly now of no more danger than a cooking haunch of venison. And, thinking of venison, unlike so many other monsters, this one smelled as if its meat would be tasty. That made me smile even more broadly.

With a wolf on either side of me, both of them wagging their tails at the pleasant smell, we came close to the tree and looked inside. It wasn't possible to tell exactly what the creature inside had been. The fur and much of the skin had been burned from its body by the great heat of the lightning and the fire it left burning in its wake. The big creature was shaped a bit like a squirrel, but much, much larger, with impressive claws as long as my fingers on its blackened paws. The lightning strike seemed to have hit it in the head, bursting open its skull. Its dead mouth hung open, displaying some very sharp teeth.

The monster had built a nest of some sort inside the hollow tree using brush and sticks. It made for an excellent cooking fire. The fat on its body sizzled and popped as it simmered.

It took a while for the fire to burn down enough for us

to get at the meat. Of course, before we ate I gave thanks. I looked up at the sky in the direction where I had heard the last rumble of thunder.

"Bedagi, Grandfather Thunder Being," I said, "we thank you for protecting us and for giving us such a fine meal."

Then I tore two big pieces of meat from one of the back legs of the creature. I fed them to Malsumsis and Wigowzo, who had both been sitting patiently with long strings of drool coming from their jaws. Then I tried some myself. This cooked monster meat tasted good.

All three of us ate until our stomachs were sticking out. Then I sat down in front of the cave with my back against the hillside. My two wolf friends curled up in front of me. I was happier than I'd felt since before that embarrassing scene at the campfire in Valley Village when Dojihla had exposed my owl ears to the people and called me a monster.

I felt around inside me for the pain that had struck at her rejection. It was still there, sharp as a small pointed stick, but it no longer made me feel lost and blind. I would never stop caring for Dojihla, even if there was no way she would ever care for me. But I was doing something now, something I knew to be good. That we had already found one wolf from my friend's lost pack told me my trail was right. The way the Thunder Being had just helped was further proof.

I looked at Wigowzo. I would try to find out from her why she was alone and where the rest of her family might be found. But not right now. The young white wolf was sleeping, her head resting on Malsumsis's dark back.

Of course, my faithful wolf companion was not asleep.

Although he was curled up with his head on his paws, his eyes were open and his ears were pricked up. He now had two friends to protect. He knew, happy and full and resting though we might be, we were never completely safe in this dangerous valley.

CHAPTER 28

Wigowzo's Story

By the time the sun was in the midst of the sky, we had reached the far edge of the forest. Nothing had troubled us, attacked us, tried to stop us. But we knew that there was still danger ahead.

My wolf friends flanked me as we loped through the forest. Even though she had known us less than a day, it was as if Wigowzo had always been with us. She'd seen how Malsumsis always turned to me, and I was clearly now the leader of our little pack.

Malsumsis looked over at me. From the other side, Wigowzo did the same.

What now? they were asking.

I looked more closely at the white wolf. She was thinner than Malsumsis. It would take more than one monster meal to fill out her lean sides. But she had a lanky strength and kept up with us easily. Now and then, just as Malsumsis did, she had ranged just a stone's throw ahead or had dropped behind, scouting for danger. But each time she and Malsumsis came back to take their place by my side, they'd given me the same message.

No enemies yet.

We were alert and ready. In fact, we were eager for a fight. That may be why none came to us. Cowards do not like to attack those who are strong and rested and prepared.

Although they'd moved with fierce determination along the trail, my two wolf friends had yelped and played together like two puppies before we started out that morning. I understood why. Malsumsis had not seen another wolf since he was that small puppy that I rescued from the Greedy Eater. And from what I had learned from Wigowzo, such carefree play had not been a part of her life in this valley.

The story that she gave us was a grim one. She told it not with words as humans speak, but in the way that wolves communicate, thoughts touching, carrying pictures and memory and emotions. I saw her pack overwhelmed by what seemed to be a pale cloud. It had confused their thoughts, commanded them to follow that trail over the ridge and into this valley. I saw them tied, shared the feelings of pain from being beaten by a shape that swirled like that cloud which had captured them. There was a shape within that cloud. It never allowed itself to be seen directly. But it seemed like that of a tall, bone-thin human being.

Hunt for me, it commanded. They had hunted.

Pull my sled as my dogs. They had done that as well.

Amuse me with your pain. That too.

But they had not done so immediately.

Two wolves, who had been the leaders of their pack, had resisted. They'd refused to move, even though pain washed over them when they did so. It had not been easy, but they'd forced themselves to defy Her. Their spirits were strong. They could not fight with their jaws, they could not flee, but they could tell their legs not to move as wave after wave of a cloudy, half-seen fire swept through them. They could be wolves. They stared straight at the one who tried to command them. They saw Her. They refused Her. Finally their bodies grew limp and their eyes closed in death.

Wigowzo and the others lacked the strength of their dead pack leaders. They'd never been able to look directly at that being which possessed such twisted power. They did as they were commanded. They hunted. They stood guard outside a lodge made of twisted stumps and vines deep in that barren land at the far end of the wide valley. They pulled the sled on which She rode, pulled it not just through the snow of winter, but also across the dry, dusty, burned land where no trees grew.

They had little to eat, just enough to stay alive. They were beaten for no reason. And being forced to do those things that they did not want to do was the hardest of all. It wore them down as the seasons passed.

She had been born here and was the youngest in their pack. No other little ones had come to the pack here in the wide valley. So their numbers had grown smaller, not just from the loss of their two leaders, but from the deaths of three of the older wolves whose bodies and hearts gave out as one season of captivity followed another.

Wigowzo and the other wolves had, in their own way, also refused to be tamed. They'd kept a spark of spirit burning deep in their hearts. The one who tried to own them saw that and so at night they'd been roped to posts, jaws tied shut to prevent their escape while the bad-minded being slept.

Escape. That was all they could think of whenever their minds were not claimed by She who made them prisoners. And finally one night when the rope about her muzzle was tied less firmly than usual, Wigowzo had managed to chew through the rawhide that bound her. There'd been no time to free the others. Night was almost over. With the first light of day, the one who held them would wake. Then there would be no chance to get away.

Run, young one, the rest had silently urged her.

So she ran. And so we found her.

The images in her mind showed me the small plan she'd made. Sneak back at night. Chew free the ropes that bound the others. Close her jaws around the throat of the bad-minded one who did them such wrong. Taste hot blood as she bit hard and shook death into that being.

It was a plan I understood. Had I been her, I would have felt much the same way. Of course I knew, as Wigowzo knew, that she had little chance of succeeding on her own.

But she was not on her own now.

I squatted beneath the last of the tall trees to study the trail that led on beyond the woods. Malsumsis and Wigowzo flopped down on their bellies on either side of me. Our journey through the forest had been the easy part. What lay ahead of us now were the swampy lands.

There were fresh tracks in the moist earth. They led into

the swamp. Two very different creatures had made these tracks—creatures we hadn't met before. One set looked like the splayed prints of a lizard with occasional marks from the drag of a long tail. The other set was like some sort of cat, rounded and with no sign of any claw marks. But those two sets of tracks were not those of an ordinary lizard and cat. They were too big. Much too big.

From the look of those tracks, these two beings had been staying just ahead of us, now and then turning to look back before continuing on toward the big swamp into which the trail now led.

From the mountaintop where I first saw it, the swamp had seemed broad but flat and featureless. Now that we were at its edge, I realized it was not so. It was a maze of bushes and twisted trees. None of the trees were tall, but they were broad-rooted. Hummocks of grass rose up out of stretches of water so dark and clouded, it was impossible to know if it was shallow or deep.

The way we planned to go led through it all. I knew the trail could be traveled. Wigowzo herself had just followed it out of that swamp only a day before. Some of her own tracks had been on that trail—overlaid here and there by those of the two very big creatures that preceded us into the swamp. They had been following her scent, but turned around when they realized she was not alone.

Without a doubt, they were lying in wait for us somewhere in that threatening tangle.

Hoo-hooo.

This was going to be interesting.

CHAPTER 29
Into the Swamp

I DID NOT LIKE SWAMPS. I didn't like them when I was an owl and I could fly over the top of them. I liked them even less now that I was a human and had to wade through them.

The dark water smelled of rotting things. Not good. Squishy stuff would get into my moccasins and stick between my toes. Not good at all. Then there were the two hungry monsters lying in wait, eager to attack and kill me. Well, at least I had something to look forward to.

By now there were no tracks to follow. The trail was under ankle-deep water. The mud beneath was firm enough not to swallow us up, but too soft to hold a distinct print. In any case, I couldn't see more than a finger's width down into the brown water.

However, I had no doubt that it would be easy for us to

locate those two monsters that had gone into the swamp ahead of us. It is very easy to locate a large, bloodthirsty creature when it attempts to tear out your throat. Just as this giant lizard was doing right now!

"HISSSSSS!"

It launched itself at me from its hiding place among the thick hummocks of grass by the trail. I ducked down so low that my face went into the water. Yuuucchhh! But the creature went right over me to land with a huge splash in the deeper water on the other side of the trail.

I'd been expecting that attack. Malsumsis and Wigowzo had made me aware of the creature's location before we reached that wide swath of thick brown swamp grasses. Standing in front of me to stop my progress, Malsumsis had whined.

Danger. Just ahead.

Wigowzo had placed herself next to him, her head pointing in the creature's direction. Squinting my eyes, for the light of the Day Fire was bright as it reflected off the water, I'd made out the shape of a long brown tail coiled around one of those hummocks of grass. It was just a few paces ahead of us.

I'd motioned for Malsumsis and Wigowzo to wait. Then I'd strolled ahead, acting as stupid as a baby duckling swimming across a pond full of snapping turtles. Monsters are seldom suspicious of stupid behavior from humans. They've grown to expect it.

My plan worked even better than I had hoped. The water the giant lizard landed in was very deep. It floundered about, trying to get its feet under it to leap at me again. But even though the creature looked to be at least twice as large as I was, its gaping mouth big enough to swallow me whole, it could not reach the bottom. Instead, it just raised its large green head higher out of the water, making it an excellent target for . . .

WHONK!

Head Breaker. It was a good solid blow, but it didn't finish the job. Not only was Big Lizard's head bony and thick, it was floating in the water. So my first blow, while painful, just knocked it back under the dark surface. A moment's pause. Then a large, yellow, splay-toed foot emerged from the water to grasp the hummock of grass next to my leg. I stepped back as it heaved its head and its other front foot up. With one sudden surge it was out of the water and onto the trail. It had moved rather more quickly than I had expected. I took several rapid steps backward, trying to stay on the solid trail and not slip off into deeper water. But Big Lizard did not follow. Instead, as it tried to pull itself forward, it failed to move.

It is hard to advance when two large and determined wolves have just grabbed your tail firmly in their teeth. Big Lizard began to swing its head back. It was, I suppose, still slightly stunned from my first blow, which had put a noticeable dent in its skull. It seemed to forget that Head Breaker and I were still there. Time for a gentle reminder. I stepped forward and made our presence known with an upward swing aimed at its jaw. Hoo-hoo!

THWACK!

I suppose my three additional bone-crushing blows along its spine were not needed, even though it was still twitching its tail. Nor was it absolutely necessary for Wigowzo and Malsumsis to rip out its throat. But it made us feel better.

The only problem with our destruction of Big Lizard

was that we made a bit of noise doing it. Malsumsis's and Wigowzo's loud battle growls and my occasional Hoo-hoos were, I am certain, heard for a considerable distance. I suppose we no longer sounded like foolish, unwary prey.

As a result, we made our passage through the rest of the swamp with nothing larger than a mosquito attacking us. That was disappointing.

In the mud on the other side of the swamp, we found the tracks of that large cat creature, as well as that of at least one other with large webbed feet. Those tracks led away from the swamp. The webbed ones were spaced so far apart that it seemed this creature was running as fast as it could. I looked a little closer at those webbed tracks. They were familiar. I had seen them before.

I started chuckling. My old acquaintance Toad Woman was surely the one who had made those tracks. And from the look of her hasty stride, she was heading as far and as fast away from us as she could go. Perhaps she would find another valley beyond this one, one that was even more safely far away from either disagreeable owls or human warriors who (in spite of their best effort) still hooted like owls when they were excited.

I did not chuckle for long. We were out of the swamp, but not out of danger. The tracks of that cat creature led out onto a wide plain. It rippled with small hills and ridges, but there were no trees. The land that rose up before us from the marshy edge of the swamp was gray with ash. Everything had been scorched more than once by fire.

I placed my hand on Malsumsis's back as he leaned against me. Somewhat to my surprise, Wigowzo came and leaned against my other side. I was fully accepted now as her pack leader, as her friend. They both stared out at the wide dead plain before us. They saw, as I did, a cloud of dust in the distance that seemed to be growing closer.

"Be ready," I said.

The low-rumbled growl that came from both their throats assured me that they were.

CHAPTER 30

No Human Can Resist

THERE WAS NO WIND, BUT each time our feet touched the earth a little puff of ash came up. This land was covered by ashes. But it was not a lifeless land. Here and there, as they always do, grasses and other small plants were beginning to grow up. If no other fire swept through here, this plain would flow again with grasses. Animals and birds would return. But not now.

The ashes looked almost like dirty snow. It was slippery under our feet. We took only a few more steps before we stopped. There was no point in going any farther. That cloud of dust was continuing to grow larger and closer. I squinted my eyes, trying to see whose swift passage across the burned plain was raising that dust cloud.

At last, when it was twice the distance of an arrow shot

away, it was close enough for me to make out figures. What I saw first were wolves. Thirteen of them had been harnessed and tied together to pull a sled much like the ones I had often watched humans slide on top of the snow. A tall figure, so bent and gray that it looked almost like a heron, stood on that sled being pulled by the wolves. In one hand it grasped a long rope tied to the leads of the wolves. In the other hand was a whip. The tall figure used that whip to strike at the bleeding flanks of the wolves and make them run faster.

Now I could hear, above the panting of the wolves and the swish of the sled, that tall being's high, hard voice.

"Bemawomahla, kagawmahla!" it shrieked. *Run, run all day!*

Close behind that sled loped the creature that had made those cat tracks. It looked something like the long-tail that hunts at night, but its chest was deeper. It was so much larger, it would have made a normal mountain lion look like a bobcat next to it.

Like the bobcat, this creature had a short tail. Unlike either of those common cats, this beast had two great fangs that hung down from its upper jaw. Each of those spearlike teeth was the length of the front part of my arm.

Malsumsis and Wigowzo were growling loudly now. I understood the anger they were feeling at seeing their relatives tied and treated with such cold cruelty. They were ready to tear that tall figure from the sled.

"Wait," I said in a soft voice.

Heeding my word, my two friends crouched down. They would wait, but they were ready to leap forward in a heartbeat.

I knelt down myself, leaning Head Breaker against my knee. I unslung my bow from my shoulder and fitted an arrow to the string. The wolves pulling the sled were so close now that I could see how thin and worn they were, how their eyes were bloodshot, and how their feet bled. The anger within me grew, but I waited. Knowing when and where to strike is something every owl has learned by the time it grows to adulthood.

"Hoooo-hooo," I whispered under my breath.

The tall being pulled back on the reins when the sled was only a stone's throw away. The wolves skidded to a stop and flopped down on the ruined earth, so exhausted that they did not try to shake their coats free of the ash that rose up and settled on them. The spear-toothed cat stopped also. It slowly lowered into a half crouch. Its small tail swished back and forth as it stared at us with a mixture of hunger and disdain.

The tall being pushed back the hood from its head. What it disclosed was a face that might have been that of an old human female had it not been so thin and bony, had its eyes not been so large and black, its teeth so sharp. I knew I was looking at the one who ruled this sad place. Winasosiz. The Oldold Woman.

The bony creature's mouth opened wider as she smiled. She raised one arm to point a clawed finger at us.

"More wolves to pull my sled," Winasosiz cackled. Then she pointed that finger at my chest. "Human food for my pet to eat."

I raised up my bow and began to pull back the arrow.

As I did so the Oldold Woman held her clawed hands out,

palms spread open wide. Her voice grew softer, smooth as the flow of thick sap from the torn bark of a pine tree.

"You cannot move," she whispered. "You cannot think."

Something washed over me. Its touch, not just on me but inside me, was like that of icy water. Yet it did not stick. I thrust it away from me with one flap of the wings within my mind. *No one tells an owl what to do!* I drew my arrow back farther.

"You are weak," she said, her voice growing louder. "You do not have the strength to hold your bow."

"Are you sure of that?" I said, drawing my arrow back to my cheek and taking careful aim.

I looked straight at the evil face of the Oldold Woman. She had ruined this land just to make it easy for her to have her sled pulled across its ashy surface. I could read that thought in her mind now. It was a thought accompanied by other thoughts. She and the terrible creatures she commanded would destroy the rest of this valley. Then they would move on to the next valley and the next. They would not stop until every place was as burned and dead as her greedy heart. Her great power had twisted her. She hated all life, longed to destroy it all.

"No human can resist me!" she snarled.

A smile came over my face. *But what about a human who used to be an owl?* I pulled my arrow all the way back.

As I refused her command, I saw something in her face that I felt sure had not been there for a long time. Uncertainty.

"Let go of your weapon!" she screamed, waving her clawed hands in frustration. *Poor choice of words,* I thought.

"Like this?" I said, releasing my grip on the bow string.

With a twang my arrow sped from the bow, burying itself

deep in the shoulder of Spear-tooth. The huge cat lurched to the side, then turned back in my direction—just in time to catch my second arrow in the center of its chest.

I am sure that arrow struck into its heart, but Spear-tooth did not die. It stumbled, then tried to gather its feet under it to leap. Before it could, it was attacked by Malsumsis and Wigowzo, who both went for its throat. Spear-tooth rose up on its haunches, trying to claw at them. Then it was buried by an avalanche of gray fur and flashing teeth. Even though they were still tied to that sled, those wolves remembered they were wolves. My defiance had weakened the Oldold Woman's control over them.

All of this happened in less time than it takes for a stone thrown high into the air to return to the earth, but when I turned my eyes to the sled, the tall figure was gone.

There was a sudden cracking sound behind me. Something came snaking in around me, knocking my bow from my grasp and drawing blood from my wrist. Another crack and a wave of fire cut across my shoulder, driving me down to one knee.

I turned to look up. Oldold Woman stood there, her arm raised to strike at me again with her rawhide whip.

"I am Winasosiz," she cried. Her voice was shrill as a storm wind.

She swung her arm forward, aiming at my face. But I rolled backward and this time her blow only struck the dusty soil, raising a cloud of ash.

"I will destroy you," she screamed, leaping forward to strike yet again. Fast as her whip arm was, my other arm, which had grabbed Head Breaker, was faster. The whip wrapped itself around my upraised club. I yanked hard and the whip tore free from her clawed fist. She stood there, staring at me with her huge dark eyes. This could not be happening. No one could defeat her.

Poor Winasosiz. She was so stunned that I think she did not even realize that the fight between the wolves and her very dead Spear-tooth had now ended. She did not notice that the wolf pack had gnawed free of their ropes. She was slowly being surrounded.

"I am Winasosiz," she cried one final time. Her voice lacked conviction.

"Hoo-hooo!" I said. "I am Wabi."

I had intended our little discussion to be longer. However, it was cut short—as was the life of that evil being—by the teeth of Malsumsis and Wigowzo and the rest of their angry relatives.

CHAPTER 31

The Old Mother Wolf

PERHAPS THAT EVIL BEING'S FLESH tasted as foul as it smelled, for after they had finished killing her, all of the wolves moved back from her body. I looked down at Winasosiz, the powerful being who had brought so much suffering to this wide valley. Her long clawed fingers were clutched against her chest, as if trying to still grasp some small part of that awful strength that had made it possible for her to control the lives of others. All she held now was her own death.

Perhaps she had been human once and had become changed and twisted by all that power. Perhaps she was some other being that simply had a humanlike shape. It did not really matter. I rolled her over with my foot so that her face was toward the earth. She did not deserve to look up at the sky. Let her dark eyes be turned to the soil.

Let her body return to the land and feed the grass struggling up through the ashes.

Malsumsis shoved his nose against my thigh. I placed one hand on his head and then the other on the head of Wigowzo as she came up to my other side. I knelt to look closely at them both, running my hands over their bodies. Malsumsis was limping, but I felt no broken bones. Wigowzo had a slash on her chest and another cut near her eye. Both cuts were clean and had ceased bleeding. Once they could wash themselves in fresh water, they would be all right.

Then I rose to look at the other wolves that had been the slaves of the evil one. Like my two friends, most had suffered wounds from the sharp claws and fangs of Spear-tooth. Two of the wolves sat on their haunches, licking wider slashes than the wounds my friends had suffered. Yet it seemed that all of the wolves would survive. Or so I thought until I saw the one wolf at the feet of two others who stood over her like guardians.

I walked slowly over to those three. Other wolves stepped aside as I did so. I could hear a murmur of wolf thoughts.

Freed us. Freed us.

Still, the two wolves who stood guard growled softly as I approached.

Malsumsis limped up to look at them.

Friend. Brother.

The two guardians stepped back. I knelt down to look more closely.

That one badly wounded wolf, whose grizzled muzzle showed her to be the oldest of them, lay on her side, panting. Her body was twisted in a way I did not like to see. I gently ran my palm over her hindquarters, feeling her back. It was broken.

Malsumsis bent his big head down to the dying old wolf and whimpered. I understood the question he was asking. Hearing it made my human eyes fill with that moisture which I now knew to be tears.

Mother?

The old mother wolf lifted her head weakly and whined back to him, her eyes holding his in a way that was so tender, it made my own heart feel as if it was about to burst.

Little One?

It had been so long. He had only been a cub, the one who fell into the river and was washed away. But Malsumsis's mother recognized his scent just as he did hers. She raised one front paw, an effort that I knew had to be hard for her, and touched his cheek with it, drawing him closer so that she could lick his face.

Happy, she whimpered. *Happy.*

Then the Great Darkness came down and spread its wings over her. Her head fell back to the dusty earth as her spirit rose from her body, her feet finding that trail of stars all wolves know to follow.

Malsumsis raised his head toward the sky and howled. Wigowzo and the other wolves joined in. Their song of loss and victory echoed across the whole of the wide valley. I raised my own head and sang with them.

As if in answer, drops of rain began to fall. Down the rain came, washing our uplifted faces, mixing with our tears, moistening earth that had been dry for too long, washing away the ashes. All around us new blades of grass glistened as bright as life and hope returning.

CHAPTER 32

The Bone Lodge

THAT GENTLE RAIN KEPT FALLING as we trotted across the land that now seemed less barren. It was not just the green of the new grass, it was also the feeling of a weight lifted from the air itself. There was still loss and sorrow here, but no longer any menace.

The wolf pack led me to the place where the Oldold Woman had lived. I did not go inside. There was nothing of that evil creature's that I wanted. It was bad enough looking at it from the outside. It was like a human wigwam, but it was even more like an upside-down nest. It was built of sticks and brush piled up and tied together by rawhide ropes. Shoved in among the brush and sticks were bones of all sizes. Many bones.

I followed the wolves to the back of that bone lodge.

Stakes had been driven into the ground. Other wolves were tied to some. There were many stakes, but only eight tethered wolves. They were thinner and weaker than those who pulled Winasosiz's sled. Before long, their bones too might have become part of the cruel one's lodge. All of them were alive, but even after I had untied them, three of the wolves could barely move. Their starved legs could not hold them up.

Another sled was leaning against one of the empty stakes. I fastened ropes to it as the wolves who had led me to this place watched. They seemed uncertain. Would I make them pull as the evil one had done?

Malsumsis barked at them. *Do not think that. Watch.*

I carefully lifted each of the three wolves too weak to move on their own. They did not resist, but it was more from their own weakness than trust of my intent. One by one, I placed them on the sled. I tied my bow and arrows and Head Breaker to the front of the sled. Then, slinging the drag ropes over my own shoulders, I turned and began to pull. It was not that hard to do. The wolves were light and the urgency I felt made their weight seem even less, even as I climbed the small hill that rose before us. At the top I turned to look back at the empty lodge of Winasosiz.

If I knew how to make fire as humans do, I thought, *I would burn that place.*

A rumble came from overhead. Then a blinding flash split the sky as an arrow of lightning struck the lodge of bones, bursting it and setting it on fire. The wolves did not run in fear from that sound, that sudden burst of light. It was as if they had expected it. They all sat on their haunches, gravely watching. Even the three wolves on the sled turned their heads to look down the hill. Though the rain still fell, that lodge burned even more quickly than dry grass. Green smoke rose from it.

"Grandfather," I said, looking up at the sky. "Thank you again."

Then I turned my back on that place and leaned into the ropes. The sled slid easily over the moist ashes and the new grass. The wolf pack, led by Malsumsis and Wigowzo, coursed around me.

When we came to the place where the body of Spear-tooth lay, I stopped. My own teeth were not strong enough and I no longer had the talons of an owl, but I had been thinking about how I could do this. I slid one of the arrows from my quiver and went down on one knee by the body of the dead monster. I had seen how large the muscles of its hindquarters were. Lots of meat there.

With the sharp arrowhead, I cut through the skin and sliced away strips of red meat as the gathered wolf pack watched. I carried those pieces of meat over to the sled, and placed one piece of meat in front of each of the three weak wolves. At first they just licked the meat, then, little by little, they ate. I went back and cut more for them.

Malsumsis and Wigowzo stood between the monster's body and the other wolves who were waiting, tongues hanging out, their tails wagging. Malsumsis looked a question at me.

Now?

"It is theirs," I said, waving my hand. "Let them eat."

Malsumsis turned and yelped at the waiting pack. In a quick gray flow, they were upon it.

Spear-tooth had been large, but the appetite of those hungry wolves was even larger. It was not long before little was left other than the creature's bones. By then, even those three wolves that had been too weak to walk were among those chewing at the monster's remains.

We rested there, but not long. I left the sled and the ropes behind when we entered the swamp. The trail seemed easier to follow now. We made our way quickly across. On the other side, again for the benefit of those wolves that had been so weakened, we rested once more.

The sun was sinking beyond the hills, but the full face of the moon was already showing. Her light would make it easy for us to travel through the night. We passed through the forest, by the lightning-blasted hollow oak—which still smelled of well-cooked meat—stopping to drink at the spring, which now held no danger. The body of the gelabago had been eaten by the birds and the few small forest creatures that had survived its hunger. Its long bones were the only hint that a terrible creature had once lived in those clear waters.

At last we reached the base of the tall range that stood between the wide valley and the home our hearts longed to see again. At the top of the ridge, we all stopped again. Our long valley had never looked so beautiful to me. I know that same feeling was in the minds of those with me.

Malsumsis sat down, raised his head up to the sky, and let out a long, beautiful, ululating howl. One by one, the other wolves joined in, filling the night with their song of return.

Happy as I was, I had a sudden feeling of uncertainty. Something seemed wrong. What was that in the patch of soft earth in front of me? I knelt beside it. The bright light of the full moon showed that it was indeed a footprint. It was three times as wide and four times as long as my own spread hand. The marks of four giant claws were dug deep into the earth. That footprint had not been here when we passed this way going into the wide valley. I made out another print, then another, farther down the slope. The trail led down toward the village where my humans lived.

I lifted my hand up to feel the string of clay beads around my neck. I am not sure why I did that. They had been placed there by the old man whose name I had not learned. For some reason, even after having left the village in disgrace, I kept those beads meant to mark me as one who hunts for the people. Even though they might not want me, I would not desert them.

CHAPTER 33

The Torn Feather

I MIGHT HAVE LOST THE trail of that big creature more than once had Malsumsis not been with me. Wigowzo had stayed with her exhausted pack just below the crest of the mountain. There were signs there of creatures good to eat such as rabbits and deer. The wolf pack would come down into the valley after they had rested, hunted, and recovered their strength. The long seasons of abuse at the hands of the evil old one would take time to heal. Weakened as they still were, none of them could move as swiftly now as could my wolf friend and I by ourselves. I needed to make haste.

There were places where I found no tracks, but the scent of that big animal was strong enough for Malsumsis to keep on its trail. It had not gone on its way without stopping. We found where it came upon a small herd of deer bedded down for the night. Its speed and the fury of its attack must have been great. The badly mangled bodies of seven deer lay in the grass. It had not stayed there long. The deer were only half eaten.

We came next to the place where there had been a quiet beaver pond. I'd always liked sitting in the dead tree at its edge, watching those busy creatures as they went about their night work, building and repairing their dam and their lodge. That dam had held back one of the small streams that led down into the long river. But it did so no longer.

The light of the moon was strong enough for me to see what had happened when that huge animal passed through. The dam had been destroyed, the pond had drained out. A trickle of water rippled through the peeled broken sticks that had once held back the flow. Big tracks led through the mud to the beaver lodge, which had also been exposed when the water level fell. The big animal was clever. It would have been hard to catch the beavers when they had water to swim in. So it drained their pond.

The lodge, of course, was torn apart. That creature ripped its way down into the nest where the beavers had been no match for the hungry jaws and ripping claws. There were no longer any beavers here, only the smell of blood on the soft night wind. The tracks that came up from the mud of the former pond headed straight down the valley toward the village where Dojihla and her unsuspecting people lived.

We ran even faster after that. I did not know how long it had taken that hungry monster to destroy the beaver colony or how many other times it had paused as it made its way through the valley. My worry was that it had reached the village.

We came to the tree where my grandmother roosted, the circle of stones where I had fallen as an owl and stood up as a human being. I skidded to a stop. I felt a sudden pain deep in my chest. It was as if I had been struck by an invisible arrow. What was this before my eyes?

I could not believe what I saw. The circle of stones was gone, the earth torn up in that circle where they had once stood. The footprints of the monster were everywhere. My great-grandmother's tree had been knocked down. It lay broken on the ground, claw marks all along its trunk.

"GREAT-GRANDMOTHER!" I shouted. "WHERE ARE YOU?"

No answering hoot came back from the wounded forest around me. But I saw something that made tears come to my human eyes. There, caught on one of the broken branches of the fallen tree, was the torn wing feather of an owl. I went down on one knee and stroked that feather with a finger.

"Great-grandmother," I whispered. "I am sorry that I left you and our valley undefended."

I stood and began to run again. This was not the moment for me to roost on a branch, feeling guilty about not having been able to protect her. What I had to do now was reach the village before the creature did.

My feet thudded against the earth. I was moving almost as swiftly as an owl can fly. Small branches struck my face. Some of them cut my cheeks, but I did not pause. I was so angry now that if that monster, whatever it was, had risen up in my path I would have hurled myself at it to tear its throat out with my teeth. As Malsumsis ran along next to me, matching me stride for stride, my wolf friend felt my mood and growled in agreement.

We came around that turn where the trail rose and I could peer down at Valley Village. It was still there, undestroyed! But it looked far different this night than it had ever looked before. It glowed from the lights of more fires than I'd ever seen. Those fires made an unbroken ring all around Valley Village. I could make out the shapes of humans inside, throwing more wood onto the flames.

I sighed with relief and placed my hand on Malsumsis's head.

"They are safe," I said to him. "Somehow, they knew that the monster was about to attack. Those fires will keep it from coming into their village."

I squinted my eyes. The piles of logs and brush that had been gathered to feed the fires were not that large. They would not be safe in Valley Village for long. There was still much of the night left. When they ran out of wood, those guardian flames would die.

I scanned the darkness around the village. I did not see the big animal, but I knew it was out there somewhere, watching and waiting. It had come from the wide valley where the Oldold Woman used fire to destroy the land. This hungry beast might fear the searing touch of flames, but it had seen burning before. It knew that all fires eventually go out. When the fires grew low it would attack.

I looked again into the village. Men were standing around inside that circle. They held bows and spears. They were watching and waiting. But that circle was large and those armed men few. How could they know where the beast would strike? Could they be sure that their arrows and spears would fly true?

"Wait here," I said to Malsumsis. "Watch."

Then, my bow and quiver slung over my shoulder, Head Breaker in my hand, I went down the hill to Valley Village.

CHAPTER 34

The Circle of Flame

UNLIKE THAT MONSTER WHICH ROAMED somewhere in the woods around Valley Village, I had no fear of fire. I could easily have leaped over that circle of flame around Valley Village. But I did not like the idea of having arrows shot at me by men ready to attack anything that tried to break through. I stopped just outside and called out loudly enough to be heard over the roaring crackle of burning logs and brush.

"NIDOBAK," I shouted, "MY FRIENDS, LET ME ENTER."

One whose hearing was that of an ordinary human might not have heard how the humans on the other side of the fire reacted to my words.

"Who is that?" a man's nervous voice said.

"Should we let him come in?" said another man.

"Perhaps it is a trick," a third man said. His voice was even more uncertain than the first man's had been. In spite of the danger, I smiled. It was the large young man who had tried to be my friend. Fat Face.

"NIDOBA, FAT FACE," I shouted again, "IT IS WABI!"

"I know that voice," a fourth person said. His tone was not uncertain, but grave and clear, that of a man whose years had given him wisdom. It was Dojihla's father, Wowadam.

"It is indeed Wabi, great-grandson of Nadialid," Wowadam said. "Make an opening! Let him enter."

Almost immediately, the section of the fire in front of me began to move. The fires were burning so hot that no one could approach them too closely, but the men had fashioned poles of green wood, three times as long as a man is tall. They were using them to push and pry the brush and logs to the side to make an opening. It was hard work. Those poles were so heavy that they could only lift them with difficulty and then drag them by one end. Hard and hardly necessary. I could leap high enough.

I took a step back, made a short run, and jumped. I soared over that opening, over the heads of the men, and landed softly on the ground behind them.

Everyone turned to stare at me, their mouths open. *Perhaps, I just leaped a little too high,* I thought.

"Who are you?" Fat Face said, dropping the pole he had been using to shift the fire.

"You know me," I said, putting a hand on his shoulder to reassure him. "I am Wabi, just Wabi." I tapped the beads that hung around my neck. Fat Face had been close by my side when the old man had given them to me. "Remember?"

"Ah," Fat Face said, "Wabi. Wabi, ah, of course." But he did not look or sound reassured. When I lifted my hand from his shoulder he took several steps backward very quickly. A little too quickly, for he stumbled and sat down hard on the ground, his eyes still on me.

I turned toward Dojihla's father. He, at least, had a smile on his face, even though I did not understand what he meant by what he said next.

"Just Wabi and nothing more? No other name?"

"Yes," I replied. "What else?"

Dojihla's father nodded his head. "Of course. What else indeed?" He reached his hand out to grasp my forearm. "I am glad to see you."

That surprised me, considering how I had left Valley Village. Not only that, I no longer wore my headband. Though I had given them no thought at all until now, my ears—so unlike those of a real human being—were clearly visible, their feathery tips rising up above my hair. But Wowadam was not looking at my ears. His eyes held mine, looking into them in a way that told me he was really seeing me. He truly was glad I was there.

I couldn't understand that. And there was another thing I couldn't understand.

"How did you know that a monster was coming?" I asked, swinging my free arm toward the fire that was at least the work of a full day.

"We were warned," Wowadam said. "So we spent all day gathering fuel and making the fires. And it was good that we did so. Just as we finished, Majiawasos came rushing from the forest, knocking down trees. But when he saw our fires, he feared to cross them. He circled our village for half the night, roaring with anger. He just went back among the trees before you arrived."

Majiawasos. The Bad Bear. So it was a huge bearlike monster. That made sense to me. But who had warned them?

However, I had more important questions to ask first.

"Is everyone safe inside the village?"

Dojihla's father nodded. "We gathered everyone in before the fires were lit."

Relief washed over me like a gentle night wind that lifts your wings. I looked around at the circle of faces that had begun to gather as word of my presence spread. Of course, not everyone came to look at me. All around the village, people had to stay by their posts, piling on more fuel to keep the fires burning. But those who had come to look also seemed pleased to see me. All but two women, one older and one young. The older woman's face was one I recognized. It was Dojihla's mother. She and the girl beside her appeared worried.

"My husband," she said, "*all* are not gathered here inside our village."

Wowadam turned to her. "What do you mean? Everyone was told that they must stay within the circle of fire if they did not want to be caught by Majiawasos. Who would be headstrong enough to . . ."

Dojihla's father stopped talking in midsentence as the thought struck him.

Dojihla's mother nodded. She indicated the girl who stood beside her. "Peskawawon has just told me, even though Dojihla forbade her to do so. Her best friend, our daughter, slipped away into the forest before the fires were lit."

“Why would she do that?” Wowadam asked.

“She said that just making fires around us would not be enough,” Peskawawon said, her words bursting forth in a torrent like water from a broken dam. “Those fires would burn out and then we would not be safe. She said that she had to find the Village Guardian because only he could save us. Perhaps he would forgive her and come back.”

“*Who* did she go to look for?” I asked, even though, dense as I am, I finally knew.

“She went to look for you,” all those gathered around me said as one.

“After you left the village,” Fat Face said, the friendly look back again, “people began to talk about you. They realized that with your strength and skill, you could easily have done us harm if you had wished to. You were not a monster.”

“Then,” Peskawawon said, “Dojihla herself decided who you really were. And she was so sorry that she had driven you away.”

I knew then what I had to do. And an idea came to me about how I could do it.

“Which way did she go?” I said to Peskawawon.

“Toward the cliffs,” she said, motioning with her chin.

A tall old woman with a kind face was looking at me from the far end of the crowd. Her hands were held up to get my attention. But I had no time to speak with anyone else. I turned toward Fat Face.

“My friend,” I said, “I am taking your fire pole.”

I lifted it from the ground. It was made from a young ash tree. It was as big around as my wrist. Where the end of it had been used to move the burning wood and brush, it had burned off into a hardened tip that was almost as sharp as a spear.

I unslung my bow and arrows from my shoulder. I would need both hands for this.

"Here," I said, putting my club into the hands of Fat Face. "Take care of this for me. His name is Head Breaker."

Then I lifted the pole to my shoulder, ran hard, and jumped with it over the circling fire, back out into the night where Majiawasos roamed.

CHAPTER 35
The Steep Slope

I HAD TAKEN ONLY A few strides when Malsumsis leaped out of the forest at me. I almost stumbled, off balance from the weight of the fire pole, but recovered and kept running. My wolf friend joined me, running by my side as close as a second shadow.

I did not speak, but Malsumsis sensed the seriousness of my mood. We had to move quickly. We ran in a great arc, skirting the edge of the fire-circled village. Although my nose was not as sharp as that of my wolf friend, we both found the scent trail of Majiawasos, the Bad Bear, at the same time.

That scent. We'd first noticed it as we came over the crest of the mountain and stood in that pass between the two valleys. It had been faint then, but was strong now. It was the normal scent of a bear and it was not. A bear has the musky smell of earth and fur and its own sweat and the food that it eats. The Bad Bear's scent was that and much more. The wholesome smell of a normal bear was washed over by the rankness of burned hair and flesh, and decay. This creature reeked of death.

There was not just one scent trail here for Malsumsis to follow. There were two. My own weaker nose caught that second scent as well. It was the clean smell of a strong young woman, her smoke-tanned doeskin dress, her hair that was washed clean and tied back. I knew why the great creature had ceased its circling around Valley Village. It had caught the odor of one of those human creatures it sought to destroy. It was on Dojihla's trail.

Is it possible to be in love with someone and be very angry at her at the same time? Why was Dojihla so stubborn, so headstrong? Why did she fool herself into believing that I was so competent as a Village Guardian that I would always come help her village when it was in danger? Didn't she know that I was just as capable of making mistakes as any other human? I was almost as angry as I was afraid that I would be too late.

Even without the help of Malsumsis's nose, the trail would have been easy for me to follow. Whereas Dojihla had slipped through the forest on winding paths made first by deer and then by generations of humans, the giant bear had gone straight, tearing through the brush, knocking over the trees. This creature was at war with all that lived.

The sun began to lift above the cliffs in front of us. I felt its welcome warmth on my face. For the first time, I greeted it the way I had always greeted its paler sister of the night sky.

"Bright one," I said as I ran, speaking those words I had

once said as a night-hunting owl, "thank you for your light. Help me find that which I seek."

Malsumsis was a few strides ahead of me as we came out of the forest. By now I realized that the path we were following, the branch in the trail that Dojihla had taken, was a choice made by one who knew she was being pursued. The other branch in the trail led to an open area away from the cliffs. There she would have been exposed to the monster that was after her.

But the way she had chosen was different. The trail was narrower here because of the fallen stones from the cliff. Some of those boulders were so large that even the giant bear had been unable to shoulder them aside as it ran. Instead it had to go around or over them, slowing its pace. Not only that, around the next bend in the trail there were caves in the face of the cliff. I had seen them during my night flights. Sometimes bats flew out of those dark openings in the stone. Hard to catch, but crunchy and tasty. If she had reached one of those caves, perhaps . . .

"Malsumsis," I called in an urgent voice, "Stop!"

Malsumsis stopped before he went around the bend in the trail. I came up beside him, breathing in and out deeply, slowing my heart and listening to see if I would hear again what I thought I had heard.

And from around the bend that sound did come again.

THUMP, THUMP, THUMP-THUMP-THUMP WHACK!

Holding my hand out in the signal for my wolf friend to wait, I crept forward to peer around the bend in the trail. It was just as well that I was cautious. There, just around that bend, was a sudden, steep, and slippery slope. Such a steep slope would have been no problem if I had still been a creature with wings. But one with legs would have found himself sliding down headlong toward the bottom. And there, at the bottom of that slope, was Majiawasos.

The monster bear was not looking our way. Instead, standing on its hind legs, it was trying to scale the steep cliff in front of it. It was totally intent on the small figure who looked down from the mouth of a cave above it. Majiawasos was grimly silent as it slowly crawled up. Its claws dug into the stone face, catching on those same handholds Dojihla had used to scramble up to the shallow cave that was her place of refuge.

Dojihla had gone as high as she could go. She was trapped by the steepness of the stone overhang above her. But, in her usual determined way, Dojihla was not waiting for the monster to reach her. Instead she was pushing hard against another of the big stones at the mouth of her cave. One more shove and it went rolling down.

THUMP, THUMP, THUMP-THUMP-THUMP WHACK!

The stone struck one of Majiawasos's paws, knocking it free from its grasp on the cliff face.

"ROWWWRRR!"

The giant bear let out a great roar that echoed back from the cliff. It slid back down to the bottom, shaking the paw that had been struck by the boulder. But it was not badly hurt. It raked its claws in fury against the broken pieces of the stone that had grazed it, scattering them in all directions. Then, once again as silent as death, it resumed its climb.

There was, I could see, only one more stone that might be pushed down. It looked far too large for Dojihla to move. Even though she was leaning against it with her back, pushing with both her legs, her face flushed from the strain, that stone did not want to budge.

There was only one thing I could think to do—if you could call what I did next a thoughtful action.

"HOOO-HOOO," I shouted.

My call was so high, so loud that both Dojihla and the monster bear turned their heads in my direction.

The look that came into Dojihla's eyes made my heart leap. She really was glad to see me.

"Wabi! I knew you would come for me!" she called. It was not just the words that she spoke, but the way she spoke them that made my heart jump even higher.

"Dojihla," I said, "stay there."

Foolish words, I know. She could not go higher and was certainly not about to climb down toward certain death. But that was all I could manage to say.

I wanted to say more. I wanted to tell her how I had always felt about her. I wanted to let her know that I longed to spend the rest of my life with her. However, my mouth could not find such words. Perhaps it was because I was not certain if I was going to survive what I was about to do. Then again, I did not have that much time for such a conversation.

But even though I could not talk, I could still act.

"HOOO-HOOO!" I shouted. The Bad Bear had stopped trying to climb. It was looking in my direction.

Then, holding the long, sharp pole firmly under my arm, I leaped forward and began to slide on my back down that steep slope.

CHAPTER 36

The Weight of the Great Bear

I KNOW THAT IT MUST have taken no more than the space of a few heartbeats for me to reach the bottom of that slope, but it seemed much longer. Sometimes things happen that way, such as when you are swooping down on a nice fat rabbit and you suddenly find yourself noticing every little detail—that the bush it has just crept out of is one of those that has yellow flowers, that there are three tall blades of grass next to the rabbit's front paws, that the rabbit is acting as if it is frozen.

But I was not swooping toward a rabbit, my wings holding me perfectly in control for the strike of my claws. The only control I had was on my gaze and the direction I pointed the sharp end of my fire stick. The great bear's paws were held wide, its own terrible claws were extended. Its gaping mouth showed yellow-stained teeth.

Yet the menace of that monster was not the only thing I noted in the brief moment that seemed to go on and on and on. What I saw made me feel pity for the creature that now intended to crush my bones and tear my flesh. Though the great creature's muscles still rippled with power, it was gaunt and had been wounded many times. There was dead flesh around its wounds. There were burn marks all over its body. One of its eyes was missing. Its wounds were too many to heal, the rot of its body too far advanced. It was living as it died. That was why the smell of burning and rotted flesh was part of its scent.

"AHHHHWRURRR!"

Its low, rumbling roar seemed to go on forever. All that kept the great bear going was its desire to hurt other things as it had been hurt, to strike blindly against its own pain.

I knew this, for as with the wolves and the Oldold Woman, I could sense its deeper thoughts. There was an undercurrent of memory—of the beginning of its own agony when it had been captured. I felt the great bear's memories of its pain as it had struggled to break the bonds that held it while the evil Oldold Woman tortured it for no reason other than her own amusement. Then, one night, it had torn itself free and fled. It had made its way across the swamp, through the forest and up the mountain, coming into this valley to escape. However, although it had escaped, it was not free. Its body was on fire with a pain that never left. Its mind had been broken. It was mad.

This great bear, which was now so close that I could feel the heat of its breath, was not like those other monsters I had fought. Only its size made it different from other bears. Before it had been caught and tortured, its only wish had been to live as a bear lives. Now the only thing that would heal its tortured spirit would be to release it from its body. To kill the bear would be an act not just of battle, but also of mercy.

That is what I thought and saw as I slid toward that giant animal that had become death walking. Then I hit the bottom of the slope. Things no longer moved as slowly as a dream. The creature loomed over me like a great black cloud in the sky. It lunged down at me as I managed to raise the long fire stick, bracing it against the rock beneath me, pointing it at the wide, fire-scarred chest.

Although that stick was not as sharp as an owl's claws, it was sharp enough. The weight of the great bear, the speed of its thrust toward me, drove the fire-hardened tip deep into its chest.

"AHWROOOO!"

It roared again then, not just in pain, but also in anger and frustration. It was being killed by my rough spear, but it was determined not to die alone. It thrust down, driving the spear deeper into its own body to reach me.

THUMP, THUMP, THUMP-THUMP.

The sound came from the cliff above us. I turned my head to look. I had been wrong about Dojihla's determination. That final stone had not been too large for her to move. It was rolling down toward the great bear and myself. We were both about to be crushed by its inexorable weight.

I felt sharp teeth sink into my shoulder and pull, just before the boulder completed its descent.

THUMP-THUMP, THUD!

Then the Great Darkness opened its wings around me. I saw and felt and heard nothing else.

CHAPTER 37
Good Medicine

WABI, YOU HAVE DONE WELL.

I knew that voice. It was my great-grandmother's, yet there was something strange about it. It seemed both close and far away, there in the darkness that held me. I felt her beak gently preening the feathers on my head. No, fingers were brushing the hair back from my forehead. Fingers?

Have you ever been in the midst of a dream and became terribly confused when you suddenly realized it *was* a dream and not reality? That is how it was for me as I struggled to wake. Was I an owl dreaming that I was a human or a human dreaming that I was an owl?

I opened one eye and saw what I was. No owl had a nose like the one I could see there in the corner of my eye. No owl was able to move its eye around in its socket the way I was now moving mine. I was still in a human body.

With that one open eye, I also saw where I was. I was inside a wigwam, the arc of bent poles covered with animal skins and tree bark above me. I tried to open my other eye, but there was something blocking my vision. I tried to lift up my arm on that side to feel what was there. A sharp stabbing pain shot through my shoulder as I did so. I could not move that arm at all. It seemed to be fastened to my chest. I struggled to sit up, but it was so hard to do. I felt dizzy.

"Be calm," said a pleasant voice from the side where my other eye could not open. I turned my head to look. A man and a woman sat there near the door of the lodge. I had the feeling they had been there for some time.

"Be calm," the man said again. I suddenly recognized who he was. It was Dojihla's father, Wowadam. "You were struck hard by some of the pieces of stone from the avalanche. But all of your injuries will heal, including your eye that is now covered to protect it."

"It is true," said the woman who sat next to him. It was Dojihla's mother. I noticed how, just like her husband, she was sitting completely still with her hands clasped in her lap. Strange.

"Olinebizon," she continued, "has assured us that you will be well and strong again. She will be back soon and tell you herself."

Olinebizon? Good Medicine? Who was that? I knew no one of that name.

I reached my good arm up to touch my painful shoulder.

As I felt it, I remembered the stab of sharp teeth just before the darkness came over me.

"Do not remove that poultice, Wabi," Dojihla's father said. "Good Medicine Woman has assured us that it will draw out the pain and help you heal." He raised a hand to gesture that I should lie back.

"Rrrrrrrrr!"

A threatening growl came from just behind my head and Dojihla's father quickly dropped his hand back into his lap.

"Your friend is very protective," he said, his voice just a little nervous. "I would say that he is a wolf were he not so much larger than any other wolf I have ever seen before."

Then Malsumsis leaned foward to look down at me and lick my cheek.

"There are only two people he will allow to touch you," Dojihla's mother said. "We can approach no closer than here by the door of the lodge."

"Despite the fact," Dojihla's father said, "that we have been ordered by a certain one of those two people—"

"No," Dojihla's mother said, "not ordered. We have been asked."

"Ordered," Dojihla's father continued, "to keep watch over you when neither one is here."

Malsumsis came around to my side. I raised my good hand to stroke his head. I noticed how he was looking at my wounded shoulder. The way he looked was almost... what? Guilty, that was it. It came to me then what had happened.

"My friend," I said, "was it your teeth I felt in my shoulder?"

Malsumsis lowered his head and whined.

Sorry.

"No," I said. "Do not be sorry. You dragged me to safety. If you had not done so, I would have been crushed." Then a thought came to me. "Dojihla?" I said, trying to sit up. "Where is she?"

Dojihla's mother carefully raised her hand. "Be calm. She is well."

"And Majiawasos, the Bad Bear, was destroyed by the avalanche that came down that cliff side," Dojihla's father said.

"When you are well and strong you can go there and see," Dojihla's mother added.

"But there will be little left to see other than bones," Wowadam added. "According to some of our young men who went to view that place, a pack of wolves came down from the mountain and has fed on the creature's body."

"Good," I said, a smile starting to come to my face. "But, wait, no one has tried to bother those wolves, have they?"

Dojihla's father laughed. "No, of course not. As long as they go their way and allow us to go ours, we are happy to share this valley with them. There has always been room for both wolves and humans. When they were gone, we missed them. It's been good to hear their songs on the night wind again."

Then I began to hear something new. It was the sound of two women talking to each other as they approached the door of the lodge.

"Ah," said Dojihla's mother, turning toward the door. "Here are the two who have been caring for you, Wabi. We will leave you in their care now."

"My dear wife means that we will leave before we are

ordered to leave," Dojihla's father said with a smile. He followed her out the door.

I was weaker than I had thought. I had to lie back down and close my good eye. I heard the two women come into the lodge and kneel beside me.

"Move aside, you," a young woman's voice said. I heard the soft pad of my wolf friend's feet as he allowed himself to be shoved back.

A hand touched my cheek and I opened my eye to look up into the concerned face of Dojihla.

"Ah," I said.

I could think of nothing more to say. It was not just because the expression on Dojihla's face was filled with hope. It was also because I could see behind her an old woman with hair as white as snow and a strange smile on her face. I had never seen that old woman before . . . or had I? And then I knew.

CHAPTER 38

Seven Stars

I REACHED MY HAND OUT toward the old woman whose smile grew broader as I did so.

"Is it you?" I said.

"Wabi," my great-grandmother answered, "here I am." She squeezed my hand in hers. Dojihla moved back slightly to allow my great-grandmother to come closer.

"Are you content to be a human?" Great-grandmother asked.

"It was good to be an owl."

"Yes, but are you content now?" she repeated.

"I think so."

I looked over at Dojihla, who seemed to be listening very intently to this conversation between us—listening as if she completely understood what we were talking about. I wondered how much my great-grandmother had told her. From what I had learned of Dojihla's stubborn nature, probably a great deal.

I nodded my head. "Yes, yes. I am content."

Dojihla let out a breath and turned her head away for a moment.

I looked toward the door of the lodge. The light of the sun was dimming. Soon it would be dark.

"Are you content, Great-grandmother?"

She smiled at that. "Wabi, don't you know how lonely I would have been without you?" She sighed. "Have you been to the place where my roosting tree stood?"

"Yes," I said, and nodded my head. It was sad to think of how the old tree had been broken.

My great-grandmother sighed again. "I have been back there too. One way or another, all trees must eventually fall. It was still standing when I changed. I saw the bear coming. I had to warn the people of the village before it reached them. There was no way they would have listened to me as an owl."

She paused then and looked out the door. "Did you see that the seven stones are also gone?"

"I did."

"They were not destroyed by that poor suffering bear. Remember the story I told you, Wabi? How they were once seven wise old ones who turned themselves into trees and then into stones? They have changed again. They have gone and taken with them the power for us to change. For better or worse, you and I are humans, and humans we will stay."

It was now dark outside the lodge. Night had come, a

night that my great-grandmother and I would never again fly through on silent wings.

I reached my good arm out to my great-grandmother. "Help me to stand," I said.

But before my great-grandmother could pull me up, Dojihla was there, lifting me to my feet. I was so surprised at her strength that I spoke without thinking.

"Am I not too heavy for you?"

"Who does this foolish one think carried him all the way from the cliff back to the village?" Dojihla said, looking back toward my great-grandmother. She wrapped my good arm around her neck and grasped me firmly about my waist. Malsumsis rose from the place he had been curled up next to the door to stand at my great-grandmother's side.

The four of us went through the door of the lodge to stand under the night sky. I turned my head to look into Dojihla's eyes. Our faces were very close to each other.

"I was afraid I had killed you when I rolled that last rock down the cliff." Her voice was soft and I saw that there were now tears in her eyes.

"No," I said, "you saved me."

"And how many times have you saved me, my Village Guardian?"

I wasn't sure how to answer, but perhaps there was nothing that I needed to say just then. It was enough to stand there with our arms around each other and the two other beings I loved most in the world close beside us.

I looked up into the sky at a pattern that I had never noticed before. There were seven stars directly overhead. Their shape was that of a circle without end.